Damaged Goods

The Redemption Series

Book 1

by

L. Wilder

The Redemption Series

Copyright 2017 L. Wilder
All rights reserved.

Without limiting the rights under copyright reserved above, no part of this publication or any part of this series may be reproduced without the prior written permission of both the copyright owner and the above publisher of this book.

This book is a work of fiction. Some of the places named in the book are actual places found in Paris, TN. The names, characters, brands, and incidents are either the product of the author's imagination or are used fictitiously. The author acknowledges the trademarked status and owners of various products and locations referenced in this work of fiction, which have been used without permission. The publication or use of these trademarks is not authorized, associated with, or sponsored by the trademark owners.

This e-book is licensed for your personal enjoyment only. This e-book may not be re-sold or given away to other people. Warning: This book is intended for readers 18 years or older due to bad language, violence, and explicit sex scenes.

L. Wilder

www.lwilderbooks.com

Cover Model: David Langlois

Cover Design: Mayhem Cover Creations
www.facebook.com/MayhemCoverCreations

Proofer / Formatter: Daryl Banner
www.facebook.com/darylbannerwriter
www.darylbanner.com

Teasers & Banners: Gel Ytayz at Tempting Illustrations

Personal Assistant: Amanda Faulkner
www.facebook.com/amanda.faulkner.1023

– In The Series –

Catch up with the entire Satan's Fury MC Series today!
All books are FREE with Kindle Unlimited!

Summer Storm (Satan's Fury MC Novella)

Maverick (Satan's Fury MC #1)

Stitch (Satan's Fury MC #2)

Cotton (Satan's Fury MC #3)

Clutch (Satan's Fury MC #4)

Smokey (Satan's Fury MC #5)

Big (Satan's Fury MC #6)

You can also check out the Devil Chasers in the new
Boxed Set!!

Dedication

To Danielle Palumbo:

Thanks for all you do!

Table of Contents

The Redemption Series

Book 1

Prologue
Nitro

Damaged people can be dangerous. They've been through hell and lived to tell about it. The pain made them stronger, more resilient, and nothing stands in their way. I'm not ashamed to say I'm damaged. I know I'm not the man that I once was. I look in the mirror, and I don't even recognize the reflection staring back at me. I no longer see a kid with hopes and dreams, living life with blinders on. He's been replaced by a man who's been broken into a shattered mess, but by the grit of his own teeth managed to pull himself back together. We all have that moment—that single moment that changes our lives forever. For some, it was something as simple as a few thoughtless words that struck a chord deep inside them, while for others, it was some traumatic event or tragedy that altered their course in a way they'd never have expected. For me, there's no question about what changed me. It was one terrible, unsuspecting night when fate reared its ugly head. Since then, my life has never been the same. I faced the pain, the anger, and the heartache. I survived it, but that doesn't mean I don't have my regrets. I should've known. I should've paid more attention, but I missed the warning signs and it cost me everything.

Ten Years Earlier

I parked my truck at the front gate of my dad's warehouse, then turned to my girl and smiled. "Sit tight. I'll be right back."

"If you're not back out here in five minutes, I'm coming in. That last glass of tea got me. I've really gotta go." Lainey smiled at me, making my chest swell with pride. I still couldn't believe she was mine. My girl was a natural beauty with her light brown hair and olive colored skin. Her eyes were as dark as the night sky, and she had a smile that could melt the coldest of hearts. She had a spirit that was wild like a mustang and a will to match. I was crazy about her, and the fact that she was carrying my kid only made me love her more. I can still remember the day I first saw Lila Grace on that ultrasound screen, all balled up with her little thumb in her mouth. Just one look at her and I thought my heart would explode right there on the spot. She was perfect, and I couldn't wait to hold her in my arms. Thankfully, I wouldn't have to wait long. Lainey's due date was only a few weeks away, which was good since our daughter was sitting right on top of her bladder.

"Three minutes tops," I promised as I leaned towards her and placed my hand on her round belly. After giving her a quick kiss on the cheek, I got out and rushed towards the warehouse.

"Hey, Nathan!"

I stopped and turned back towards the truck. She

was leaning out the window with a goofy grin on her face. "Yeah?"

"Just wanted to let you know you've got a great ass."

"Is that right?"

"Yep. One of the best."

"Glad you're enjoying the view."

I shook my head and laughed as I continued inside. My father had sent a message that he needed me, and since business was never discussed over the phone, I had to go to him to see what he wanted. When I got to his office, I expected to find him at his desk going over inventory, but instead, I found Murray, his longtime partner, sitting in his spot. He was like a second father to me, a confidant whenever I needed one, and he added a bit of much needed humor to the place. Without looking up, he motioned towards the back of the building. "Your father's out back."

"Good to see you, too."

"Um hmm," he grumbled. "We're gonna need you tomorrow."

"Figured that." Since it was the end of the month and everyone wanted their shipments out on the first, we'd have to bust our asses to get everything done on time. It was nothing new, though. It was always like that with our kind of inventory. Dealing with illegal guns meant we were always on high alert—hoping for the best, but expecting the worst. "I'll be here first thing."

"Bring coffee."

"Why? I thought that was Nick's job."

"Had to let him go."

Knowing that meant I'd be stuck doing all the grunt work they didn't want to do, I groaned, "Damn it. Why'd you go and do that?"

"The kid's got nothing going on in that head of his. He couldn't even get a cup of coffee without screwing something up." He looked up at me with one of his smirks. "Besides, why pay someone to do something you can do?"

There was no point in arguing, so I turned and started for the door. "I'll bring the fucking coffee, but I draw the line at doughnuts."

"Hmm, doughnuts do sound good. Get me a few with sprinkles."

"Fuck off, Murr. I'm not getting fucking sprinkles." I slammed the door behind me in aggravation, knowing damn well I'd get his stupid doughnuts.

I headed to the back of the warehouse and found Dad talking with the DeMarco brothers. He'd been working with them for the past few months, but he'd made it clear that his patience was growing thin with them. They'd decided to expand their small business to include prostitution, drugs, and the like. My father had warned them against it, but he'd let it ride. He had let them do their thing, until they came up late on their last shipment and came up short on their last payment.

"You're late. That's the bottom line."

"I know. We just need a little time, Pops," Joey

pleaded.

"I'm not your Pops. I'm not your bro. Until you pay me the five grand you owe and come up with the hundred assault rifles, I'm your worst enemy."

"Look, you'll get what's coming to you. You know we're good for it."

"I'll tell you what I know: Time is money, and I'm done fucking around with the two of you."

Lenny, the taller of the two brothers with a large, crooked scar along his cheek, placed his hand on my dad's shoulder. In a playful voice, he said, "Come on, Cal. Don't be like that."

"Lenny, you've got until tomorrow at noon."

"We can't have it by tomorrow. We need more time!"

"You're not getting it."

"Give us the time, Cal. Don't make us do something you'll regret."

My father took a threatening step forward. "There are two kinds of people in this world, Lenny. Those who make threats, and those who make good on them. Tomorrow at noon, or you know what will happen."

"You forced our hand, Cal. What happens next is on your head."

There was no mistaking their anger as they both stormed past me and out the back door. Once they were gone, I walked over to my dad. "Everything okay?"

As always, he was cool, calm, and collected. "Why wouldn't it be?"

"Seriously?"

"What? You mean Lenny?" He laughed. "You gotta remember something, son. This business we're in is hard. It's even harder when you're stupid. Those two idiots dug their own graves when they decided to tie up with Link."

"I thought you and Link were tight."

"I never said we weren't. Besides, I'm not talking about me and my business. We're talking about them. Those boys saw dollar signs and got in over their heads. It's gonna cost them."

"And what about us? We need that shipment."

"We'll be fine." My gut pulled at me, making me wonder if he was right, but my father's been doing this a lot longer than me. Deciding that he knew best, I left it. He started walking towards his office. "You know your mother is expecting you and Lainey for dinner tonight."

"We wouldn't miss it. We're headed that way after I leave here." I followed him into his large office and over to his desk. "I just came by to see what you needed me to do."

He reached inside his desk drawer and pulled out a thick yellow envelope. "I've got some papers that I need you to get over to Des."

"No problem. I can take care of it."

"Make sure you get this done tonight. He's expecting them."

"You got it."

I started for the door and was just about to walk out

when I heard him shout. "Hey, Nate."

"Yeah?"

"Eyes and ears open."

"Always, Pop."

I was on my way back out to the truck and was about to open the door when Lainey came rushing inside. She stormed past me and headed straight for the restroom. Just before the door closed behind her, she shouted, "Just so you know, that was not three minutes."

When she finally came back out, I smiled and said, "Sorry about that, baby."

"It's all good. I'm better now." She gave me a quick kiss before she turned and started for the door. "Let's roll, Daddio. We've got places to go, and people to see."

I shook my head and laughed. "I love you, woman."

She turned back to look at me with one of her smiles that knocked me off my feet. "You'd better, because you're stuck with me."

"I'd say that makes me a lucky man."

She stopped and turned to face me, looking at me with nothing but love in her eyes. She brought her hands up to my face, pulling me close as she pressed her lips against mine. Her kiss was soft and filled with promise. I'd never dreamed I could be so content with another human being. She was my everything. "I'm the lucky one."

We got back to the truck, and we'd only gone a few

miles when I looked over and found her with her eyes closed and her head propped against the window. She was sound asleep—another side effect of the pregnancy. Poor thing was still out cold when I drove out to Desmond's place. It wasn't until I pulled up at my folks' place that she finally woke up. It was pitch dark when I finally parked the car, and I felt bad for having hauled her around all day. "Hey, baby, you have a good nap?"

She rubbed the sleep from her eyes as she yawned. "Yeah, but I need to stretch my legs and get something to eat. I'm starving."

I got out of the truck and walked over to open her door. "Come on. Mom will have dinner ready in a minute."

She followed me inside where we found my mother standing at the stove, stirring the pasta sauce. She was one of the good ones. She always had a smile on her face and worked her ass off to make sure her family was taken care of. She was one hell of a cook, and her spaghetti was legendary. "Smelling good, Mom."

"You finally made it." She spun around, spread her arms wide, and rushed over to me with a big smile on her face. "I was beginning to think you weren't coming."

"You said dinner was at 8. I'm ten minutes early."

"Well, you know I like to spend time with you." She wrapped her arms around me and gave me a tight squeeze, then headed over to Lainey. "It's been ages since you've come to see me!"

"Miss Clara, we were here on Sunday."

"Oh, that doesn't count. You were only here a few minutes," she huffed. "With Colton gone, it seems like I never get to spend time with my boys anymore."

My brother had decided a long time ago that he wanted nothing to do with the family business and had gone off to some Ivy League school out east. He hadn't come home in months, and even though my mother would never admit it, I knew it was getting to her.

"Now get this sweet girl something to drink, while I get the bread in the oven."

I looked over to Lainey and asked, "Tea or water?"

Before she could answer, Mom started fussing under her breath as she looked frantically through the cabinets. "I can't believe I forgot it. I don't know what I was thinking."

"What's wrong?"

"I can't find the bread!" She rushed over to the pantry and dug around inside. "It's not here."

"Mom, we can live without bread. It's not a big deal."

"We can't have spaghetti without garlic bread, Nathaniel."

I knew she was upset when she used my full name, and knowing she wouldn't be happy until she got just what she needed, I offered to go grab some for her. "I'll run to the store. What do you need?"

"Are you sure?"

"Yep. Just tell me what you want me to get."

She grabbed her purse and started going through her wallet. "Get us a loaf of French bread."

"I thought spaghetti was Italian," I teased.

She tried to hand me a ten-dollar bill, but I refused. "Maybe I should go with you."

"No, I'll go with him," Lainey proposed.

"You both stay here. I've got this."

Just as I opened the door, my dad stepped inside. "Where are you running off to?"

"Just a quick run to the store, Pop. I'll be right back." I gave him a pat on the shoulder and headed for my truck.

I heard the screen door open again, followed by my mother shouting, "Make sure it's fresh!"

I nodded as I started the engine and pulled out of the driveway. It didn't take me long to get to the store and back—fifteen minutes at the most. I was expecting dinner to be on the table when I walked into the kitchen, but as I walked in, I found it empty. I stopped in my tracks as a strange sensation washed over me. I'm not sure what triggered the feeling... maybe it was the unsettling silence or the hint of gunsmoke that filled my nose, but I knew immediately that something was off. As I pushed down the panic creeping into my throat, I called out to my mother. I got no response, so I called out to Lainey. Nothing.

I could hear the low rumble of the news playing on the television as I started down the hall. A nervous energy surged through me as I neared the living room. It was like I knew something awful was waiting there for me, so I picked up my pace and called out to mom once again. Still I got no response. When I finally made it into the living room, my entire world suddenly crashed down around me. I stood there frozen as I looked at my father sprawled across the floor, blood gushing from his lower abdomen and his left temple. My mind couldn't comprehend what my eyes were seeing. It didn't make sense. He had been fine just a few minutes ago, smiling as I greeted him at the door. I rushed to his side, praying that he was still alive. I quickly rolled him over only to find his expression was blank and his eyes were wide open, staring at the ceiling. My breath caught in my throat as I realized the man I had always thought was indestructible was gone.

Panicked, I quickly turned behind me and found Lainey crouched down on the sofa. Bile rose in my throat when I saw her body covered in blood. Time stood still as I sat there staring at her. Several seconds passed before I was finally able to force my body to move towards her. My feet felt like lead weights as I staggered over to the sofa. I reached for her, pulling her into my arms as I cradled her lifeless body close to my chest. The world around me faded away as I looked down at her beautiful face. A cloud of darkness fell over me as I rocked her back and forth in my arms, all the while praying that it was all some kind of mistake. I tried bargaining with God, pleading with him to exchange my life for theirs, but my prayers weren't answered. My family was gone, ripped away, leaving me completely lost and broken. I rested my hand on her stomach, thinking of the daughter I'd never get to hold in my arms. Thoughts of the ultrasound, the baby clothes, the nursery, and all the hopes and dreams we'd shared came crashing through my mind. My future faded before my eyes, and I'd never felt such a pure, all-consuming pain. Guilt crept over me as I berated myself for not being there when they'd needed me. My tortured cries echoed through the room as I pulled her closer, begging them both to forgive me. I would've still been sitting there holding Lainey in my arms if I hadn't heard my mother groaning in the corner.

"Mom?" I hurried over to her and was overcome with relief as she reached her hand out to me. "Don't move. I'm calling for help."

She was losing so much blood, but she managed to grasp on to my arm as I called 911 and then Murray. Once I was done, I looked down at her and tried to reassure her. "They're on their way. Just stay with me."

With a grimace, she sighed and closed her eyes. I took the blanket off the back of the sofa and used it to apply pressure to her wounds, hoping to slow the bleeding. We were still waiting on the ambulance when Murray came crashing through the front door. The blood drained from his face as he looked around the room.

He dragged his hands down his face as he shouted,

"Oh god. No!"

The next few days were a blur. After burying my father, fiancée and daughter, I was constantly at the hospital with Mom or dealing with the cops. They had more questions than I could ever begin to answer, and I was losing my patience. I already knew in my gut who'd killed my father and Lainey. I just hadn't figured out how they'd done it. Dad's security system was the best around, along with several guards monitoring everything coming and going. He didn't leave anything to chance -- always making sure his family was safe, so it didn't make sense that someone had been able to break in so easily. It wasn't until days later that we found out his security system had been down for an update, leaving the house and gate completely unmonitored. The guards never saw them coming and once they were killed, the house had been left completely unprotected.

Once we were certain that Mom was going to pull through, I asked her about the shooting. After showing her several photographs, she quickly confirmed our suspicions about the DeMarco brothers, and Murray and I set out to take our revenge. I'd like to say that we found them and made them pay for what they'd done, but that never happened. They both vanished that night, leaving my need for vengeance unanswered. A void filled my chest, destroying the carefree, easy-going man I used to be. That man failed the people he cared most about. He was gone, leaving me forever cold and bitter.

I would never look to the future: there'd be no more hopes and dreams... That time in my life was done. I would be forever haunted by my past. It consumed me, and my need for revenge was the only thing that kept me going. I wouldn't rest until they paid for what they'd done. I was damaged through and through.

Chapter 1
Nitro

I'd been running guns with the brothers of Satan's Fury, one of the most notorious MC's in Washington, for as long as I could remember. It was a profitable venture for us both, until everything went to shit. I'd like to say the blame fell on someone else, but it was me—*all me*. Big, one of the brothers and a close friend of mine, had come to me for help when one of their girls came up missing. They soon discovered she'd been kidnapped by the cartel and was to be sold in one of their sex-trafficking auctions. The MC had connections, more than most, but not the kind they needed—not this time. They were dealing with the fucking Mexican cartel. Knowing the last thing they needed was an all-out war, they came to me. The brothers knew with my line of work I had ties with people from all over the world, and they hoped I'd be able to call in some favors to bring her back home. I agreed to help them even though I knew I was putting my life and theirs at risk.

I touched base with my contact and managed to get my foot in the door. I knew enough about sex-trafficking to know that I didn't want any part of it. Just the thought of buying a chick as some kind of sex slave made my stomach turn, but there I was, standing in the middle of a basement in California doing whatever I could to be the highest bidder. It wasn't at all like I'd expected it to be. It was much, much worse. The room was dim, except for the lights shining down on the girls, and it was filled with a thick cloud of smoke, making it difficult to breathe. I glanced around the room, and I was repulsed at the sight. These men had money. They could date any woman they wanted, but they wanted more. These men wanted a possession—a woman they could own in every way—and the cartel gave them the means to do it. Reeking of arrogance, the predators stalked around the room as they checked out their prey, all the while chattering back and forth amongst themselves like they were old friends. Fucking assholes. I hated even being in the same room with the obnoxious pricks. Being close to them was getting harder by the minute and making me feel like the walls were closing in around me.

While they were living it up and enjoying every moment, I took a step back and remained silent, trying to play it cool—trying to hide my absolute repulsion at the whole thing. I just didn't get the appeal. Not only were the women dressed in tired-ass bikinis that were two sizes too small, they were also drugged out of their minds, barely aware of what was going on around them. Hell, they even had some kid in the mix. She couldn't have been more than twelve years old. It was sad and demoralizing, and I wanted to get the hell out of there. Unfortunately, I wasn't going anywhere, not until I got their girl back.

Everything had gone as planned. I'd pulled every string that could be pulled to get us into the auction. Now, I just had to outbid the others and bring her home—simple enough. It was a good plan, but there was just one problem. With just one look, she became my obsession, an obsession that stirred something deep inside, and I had to have her. I couldn't explain it. Sure, she was beautiful, but she wasn't your typical blonde haired, blue eyed beauty. There was something different about her. She stood there staring at me with those gorgeous, dark blue eyes, and even with the drugs, they pierced right through me. Life had thrown her some curves, but she was still standing. There was a strength inside of her, a strength that I needed to put back the pieces of my shattered soul. I knew right then and there that she was the key to my salvation.

I placed my bids not only for Tristen, but for the young girl, too. There was no way I was leaving either of them there. Once I'd won and my debt was paid, we got the hell out of there. Cotton, the president of Satan's Fury, expected me to bring Tristen home, but that wasn't going to happen. Instead, he'd be getting the kid. I should've talked it out with him and respected him enough to try to work things out, but I was impatient. I knew it would cost me later, but I didn't want to waste time dealing with any bullshit. Without squaring things with Cotton, I put Tristen and her computer savvy sister, Josie, in my SUV. Taking Josie hadn't been part of the plan, but she didn't give me much choice. She'd just gotten her sister back, and she was adamant about staying with her. I didn't see the harm. Besides, if it hadn't been for her hacking into the club's computer system, none of us would've known that Tristen had been kidnapped in the first place. Once they were settled in the SUV, we headed to Arizona. Knowing the cartel had been drugging her, I decided to take Tristen to a rehabilitation center to help her deal with her addiction. The rehab facility was one of the best around, and I had no doubt they'd get her back on her feet. I'd like to say that I was doing it all for her, that I was just making sure she got the help she needed, but I wasn't doing it for her. I was doing it for me. Just like the other sick bastards back in that room, I wanted her for myself, for her to be mine in every way, and at the time, I didn't care if she felt the same. Tristen Carmichael was mine.

I knew it was fucked up. I knew it was wrong, and there would be hell to pay. I'd gone against my word. I'd double-crossed the club when I hadn't talked to Cotton, and I'd only made matters worse when I didn't bring her directly home. My actions had forever severed my ties with Satan's Fury. I knew going to Cotton wouldn't change anything, but I respected him enough to have a face to face with him. Once Tristen was done with rehab, we headed straight to the clubhouse.

When we walked into the bar, Cotton was already there waiting for us. While Cotton greeted Tristen with a smile and a hug, Big walked up behind them. I didn't miss the uneasy look he gave me as he glanced over in my direction. We'd been friends for a long time, and over the years, we'd found ourselves in some pretty tight spots. In the past, we'd always managed to find our way out, but I knew this time would be different.

Not wasting any time, Cotton told Tristen, "I'm sure the girls will be glad to see you, too. Cass and Peyton are in the kitchen. Why don't you go check in with them while we have a word with Nitro?"

Her eyes were filled with concern as she turned and looked at me. Over the past few weeks, we hadn't spent much time together. She had been busy with her counseling sessions and group therapy, so I had no idea how she really felt about things. It meant something to me that she was concerned about me, though. I gave her a nod, letting her know I was good. She didn't look convinced as she answered Cotton. "Sure. It would be great to see them."

As she walked out, Guardrail and Maverick came into the bar and gathered behind Cotton. Judging by their heated glares, I could tell that they weren't exactly happy to see me. These were men you just didn't fuck with. Ever. So needless to say, I'd found myself in a precarious situation. I'd like to say it bothered me that my old friends were looking at me like they wanted to put a bullet in my head, but it didn't. I looked Cotton in the eye as I said, "We've come to a crossroads, brother. I know you are set on severing ties between us, and I'm not here to change your mind."

"That's a good fucking thing, because there is

nothing you could do or say that would change my mind."

"Figured as much. I've known you long enough to know how goddamned stubborn you can be."

"Being fucking stubborn has nothing to do with it. We trusted you, and you stabbed us in the motherfucking back," he growled.

Anger boiled inside of me. I knew I'd fucked up by not coming to him, but in the end, I'd done right by Tristen. "I saved your girl from the fucking cartel, Cotton. Got her the help she needed to get back on her feet. If that's stabbing you in the back, then it is what it is."

"Don't try to turn this around, brother," he roared. "You fucked this whole thing up, and you know it. You had to be the fucking hero for some girl, to hell with the consequences."

"I had my reasons."

"Pussy isn't a fucking reason to turn your back on the club."

Rage surged through me as I took a step towards him. "You're walking a thin line, Cotton. Truth is, you'd do the same damn thing if Cass was standing up there, being sold like a piece of fucking meat."

"I wouldn't have double-crossed the brothers."

"You're a goddamned saint, Cotton." He was being a self-righteous asshole. "Never had any fucking regrets. Must be nice to walk around in those fucking boots of yours." I shook my head in aggravation. There was no point in trying to talk this thing out with him. He was too thick-headed to listen. "There's no sense in continuing this bullshit. What's done is done."

"Couldn't agree more." Cotton's expression was full of hate as he nodded towards the door. "Nothing keeping you here."

"If you're ready for me to go, then get Tristen back in here. Ask her yourself and see what she really wants to do. If she chooses to stay here with you and keep the life she had, then I'll walk out of here and never look back. But if she decides to go with me, then I'm taking her. Either way, this shit ends today."

Cotton turned to Big and ordered, "Go get her."

He turned and headed towards the kitchen. Tension crackled around the room as we waited for them to return. It was fucked up that our ties ended over all of this, but there was no going back. And honestly, I wouldn't have changed a damn thing.

There was no doubt Tristen was nervous as she walked over to Cotton. "Big said you wanted me."

"I do." He stepped towards her and placed his hand on her shoulder. "Need to know what you want to do."

"About?"

"Do you want to come back here and stay at the club... or do you want to leave here with *him*? The choice is yours, doll."

My nerves got the best of me as I waited for her to answer. I hoped that she wouldn't have any doubts, but she'd be crazy not to. She didn't know a damn thing about me, and there was no real reason for her to leave. She had gotten better. She didn't need me, and I was worried she might end up staying. I had my doubts until she looked over at me. There was something in her eyes that let me know her answer before she even said the words. "I'll never be able to thank you for all you've done for me, Cotton. I don't know what I would've done if you hadn't let me stay here. All the brothers have been good to me, and I love all of you... but I don't belong here anymore."

"You sure about this?"

She glanced over at me once more. "I am. This is something I need to do."

"You've gotta do what's right for you, Tristen. I get that. Just know the door is always open."

"Thank you, Cotton." Tears ran down her face as she gave him another hug, then she turned to me. "I guess I better go get my stuff."

Once she was done packing, her sister helped us load her things into the SUV. We said our goodbyes, then drove out onto the highway, leaving the brothers of Satan's Fury behind. On the way back to my place, Tristen was quiet. I figured she was sorting through the chaos in her head and trying to convince herself that she'd made the right decision in leaving. I'd made her think she'd had a choice, that it was up to her if she stayed at the club or left with me, but the truth was I'd never intended to leave that clubhouse without her.

"Cotton looked mad," Tristen muttered as she

stared out the window.

"He was."

"Was he mad at me?" Her voice trembled with worry. "He's done a lot for me... I really don't want him to be mad."

"He's not mad at you. He's mad at me."

"After everything you did, why would he be mad at you?"

"In our line of work, you only trust the people who've proven they can be trusted. Over the years, Cotton proved that he was a man I could trust, and I'd done the same with him, until a few weeks ago. I let him down."

"Can't you try to fix it?"

"I'm not sure that's possible."

"If you proved that you could be trusted once before, you can do it again."

"Maybe, but I'm not so sure I want to."

She looked at me confusedly. "Why wouldn't you want to?"

"It's complicated."

She sighed as she turned and looked out the window. I knew she wanted more from me, but I didn't see the point in talking about it. She wouldn't understand, so there wasn't any use in trying to explain it. After several minutes had passed, I thought she'd let it go, but I was wrong. "Maybe you could try telling him you're sorry."

"I'm not sorry."

Her eyes never left the window as she muttered something under her

breath. "Either way. Apologizing isn't always about being sorry. It's just a way of showing that you care more about your friendship than your ego."

"It's not that easy," I told her, ignoring her little jab at my pride. "In any other situation, you might be right, but like I said... it's complicated."

"If you say so."

An uneasy silence filled the truck as we continued towards my condo. I'd called ahead and let Max know that we were on our way. He was my head of security and everything in between. I counted on him for just about everything, including getting things ready for Tristen. We were both exhausted from the long trip, and I figured she'd be ready to settle in. As we pulled up to my complex, I heard Tristen take in a deep breath. When I looked over, I found her staring up at the building with wide eyes. "This is where you live?"

"This would be it. I live on the top floor."

"Of course you do." She cleared her throat as she reached for her purse. "Where will I be staying?"

"I've got a spare room at my place."

"Your place?" she asked, sounding surprised.

"I figured it would be the easiest thing for now."

"Oh... okay." Her voice trailed off as she opened the door and stepped out onto the sidewalk. "I'll go grab my bags."

"I'll send someone down to get them later."

"Um… okay." Again, her voiced sounded strained, less self-assured than I'd become accustomed to.

"Something wrong?"

"No. Everything's fine." She closed the door and started walking towards the front door. Something was wrong. I could hear it in her voice, but from the way she had just bolted towards the front door, I knew she didn't want to talk about it, at least not yet.

Chapter 2
Tristen

I was losing it, completely and totally losing it. I couldn't even think straight, much less form actual words. As soon as I'd seen Nathan's condominium, my mind short circuited, and I was bombarded with doubts. In theory, leaving with him had been a good idea. I would stay with him for a few days, and then, I'd move into my own place. I'd start my new life and leave my past behind me—all of it. It was my second chance. When my parents died in that crash, part of me had died along with them. I'd lost my way and made some stupid mistakes, but in time, I'd found my footing. Cotton and the club had taken me in; they gave me a safe place to stay and a job working in the kitchen and in the bar with Cass. They'd treated me like family and I loved being there, but something had changed—maybe I'd fallen for the wrong guy or maybe it was just that I'd outgrown the club. Either way, I was ready to move on. Needing a change is what spurred my trip to Mexico. I'd thought it would be a chance for me to get away and clear my head, but I never made it to Mexico. Instead, I was kidnapped, and everything went to hell.

Once I figured out what was happening to me-- that I was to be sold off to the highest bidder, I knew what kind of life was in store for me. Like the other women they were holding captive, I was going to be someone's possession, a sex-slave or worse. When I met Lauren, a young girl they'd put in the room with me, I tried even harder to find a way out, but nothing I tried worked. There was no escaping these men, and I'd lost all hope of ever getting away. There would be no more dreaming of a better future or a better life. But then Nathan came along. Seeing the look of determination in his eyes gave me hope that I might just make it out of there. When he actually pulled it off, when he carried me and Lauren out of that god-awful place, I actually thought I might still have a chance-- that I could still have all the things I'd always wanted. But now that I was actually in the elevator with him, I was beginning to have my doubts. I blamed Mr. Johansson, my counselor for my hasty decision. The last time we'd talked, he told me to stop worrying about all the things that could go wrong and start thinking about all the things that could go right. He said I was one of the lucky ones. I'd gotten completely addicted to the drugs those men had given me. While I still had plenty of issues to deal with, I was already one step ahead of most of the people he worked with. He'd convinced me that I still had a good chance at a future I would be proud of. By the time we were done discussing all the possibilities, I'd imagined myself in a nice apartment with a great new job, and that I'd take some night classes where I'd meet all kinds of new people. I'd really psyched myself up for it. Now, my confidence was shot to hell and all those things terrified me… and I hadn't even taken into account my situation with Nathan. He was a whole other level of terrifying.

He was every girl's fantasy—devastatingly handsome, rich and powerful, and for some crazy reason, he'd decided to take it upon himself to rescue me. I couldn't deny that I was drawn to him, but I couldn't explain why. At first, I thought it was just gratitude. I'd been kidnapped, held captive and drugged, but that was just the start. I'd known what was coming, and even though I'd tried, there was no escape. I was going to be auctioned off to their highest bidder, losing my freedom forever to become some man's sex slave. I'd thought my life was over until he showed up. One look at him, and I had hope that I might just make it out. When he took me in his arms, protectively cradling me against his chest, I'd never felt so safe, like nothing could ever hurt me again. He was my hero, but he didn't stop there. He got me the help I needed to recover from my ordeal, and then offered me a place to stay until I got back on my feet. So, yeah. I was more than a little grateful.

I'd worked myself up into a nervous wreck, and by the time we reached the top floor, I thought my heart would beat right out of my chest. I took a deep breath and looked over at Nathan. He didn't smile, he didn't take me in his arms and hold me close, but something about the way he looked at me calmed my racing heart, easing the anxiousness growing inside me. When the elevator doors opened, he stepped forward and said,

"Here we go."

I followed him inside and tried to act unaffected by the enormous kitchen and all the lavish furniture. It was amazing. The modern gray and black tones of the paint and decor gave it an elegant atmosphere, but it still felt comfortable. I couldn't help but wonder if he had taken the time to pick out the beautiful abstract paintings on the walls or the fancy florals that were scattered throughout the condo. Whoever had done it had great taste. He'd obviously done well for himself, and I couldn't help but wonder how he'd made his fortune. I knew he worked with the club, and I knew the kind of lives they led. So, I could only assume it was something illegal—drug or gun trafficking... or something even more dangerous. "It's really something."

"Thanks." He started walking through the living room as he said, "Come on. I'll show you where you'll be staying."

I was eager to see my room, but I was drawn over to the giant wall of windows. The view was absolutely spectacular as I walked over to the ledge and said, "You can see the entire city from up here."

He came up behind me and looked over my shoulder, sending little shivers down my spine as I felt the heat of his breath on my neck. "Not exactly a big city out there."

"Maybe not, but it's still beautiful." A thousand thoughts rushed through my mind as we stood there looking out over all the lights, and each and every one were about him. I couldn't help myself. Every time he was close, my body would take notice with a skipped heartbeat or a quickened breath. The attraction I felt towards him was palpable. I felt it all the way down to my bones every time he looked at me. All those little reactions made me think our connection had more to do with lust than gratitude.

When he let out a deep breath and shifted behind me, the spell was broken. I turned around and smiled. "You were going to show me my room?"

"Of course." He headed down the hall and stopped at the third door. As he opened it, he motioned his hand down towards the end of the hall. "I'm the last one on the left."

"Okay."

"Just let me know if you need anything."

"Thanks." I stepped inside and was about to shut the door when I realized I didn't have my bag. "Oh. Wait. What about my things?"

"I'll have someone bring them up. If you want to take a shower, there's a bathrobe hanging in the closet."

As soon as I closed the door, I walked over to the bed and collapsed. Without taking the time to look around the room, I rolled to my side, taking the edge of the comforter with me. I balled up into a small cocoon and closed my eyes. The day had taken its toll on me, and I was completely exhausted. I just wanted to lay there and sleep for the next three days, but then the dreams started rolling in, each one worse than the last. I tossed and turned, but I couldn't pull myself out of the nightmares. I was dragged once again to the night of my kidnapping. I could feel the panic rising in my throat as I struggled to understand what my attackers were saying. I tried in vain to scream for help, but my words slurred incoherently. Darkness clouded my sight as I kept drifting in and out of consciousness. Each time I came to, disorientation and fear flooded my veins. I had no way of knowing if I was headed to my death or something far worse. The mildewed stench of the shack they confined me in filled my nostrils, and I thought I would be sick. They tied me to the rusted iron bed like an animal. In that moment, I lost hope. I knew in my gut that they were going to kill me, and I would never see my sister again. I thought of all the things I would never get to tell her... and never get to apologize for. Then more needles came. I forgot everything in a haze of delirium and shame.

The more I fought, the more tangled in the blanket I became. I could feel my heart pounding against my chest, and as the worst part of the dream began to unfold I became even more frightened, even more desperate to wake up. I could hear their laughter behind the door and their footsteps as they got closer to my room. I tried to break free from my restraints, but it was just no use. They were coming. They came over and over again... none of them willing to help me. I thrashed to my side and ended up rolling off the edge of the bed. With a loud thump, I landed face first on the floor. I groaned as

I tried to pull myself free of the covers, but I was wound too tight. Shit. With a final jerk of my elbows, I freed myself. I lifted myself up onto my knees and tried to shake it off.

Taking a deep breath, I wiped the sweat from my forehead and stood. I needed something cold to drink and to get out of the confines of that room. I had no idea what time it was, so I tiptoed down the hallway towards the kitchen. As soon as I stepped into the living room, I spotted Nathan's blue eyes staring at me. With a concerned look he asked, "Is everything okay?"

I cleared my throat and continued towards the kitchen. "Everything's fine. I just wanted to get something to drink." After opening a couple of cabinets, I finally found the glasses. I filled up a tall glass of water and headed back into the living room. I had two choices: I could bite the bullet and sit down next to him, or I could go back to my room and face the nightmares. I'd like to say it was an easy decision, but my nerves were completely shot. I wasn't sure I was prepared to handle the riotous effect he had on me. It was a risk I was willing to take. I sat down next to him and asked, "You couldn't sleep either?"

"Nah." He eyed me with a hint of annoyance as he tried to focus on the TV.

"Whatcha watching?" I asked, determined not to be banished to my bedroom.

He waited for the characters to stop speaking before he replied. "G.O.T." I stared blankly at him. "You know, the show with the dragons?"

"Um… can't say that I do," I replied, confusion clouding my face.

"You're missing out. It is pretty addictive."

I looked at the screen to see a beautiful blonde in medieval clothing ordering an execution. The smile on her face was a bit terrifying. She didn't look like anyone you'd want to screw with. "Who's that?"

"The queen. She has a thing for killing anyone who fucks with her or her kids."

"Sounds like some women I know."

"No, trust me. You don't know anyone like this chick." I sat back and watched for a few minutes. The room was completely dark except for the television screen. It was cute to see the different expressions on Nathan's face as he watched the action unfold. He was clearly way more into it than he'd let on. When a dashing blond knight came on screen, Nathan groaned. "This motherfucker."

"Who's that?"

"Her brother," he answered, giving me the side-eye.

"Uh-huh. And who's that?"

"Just watch. You'll see."

"But…" I started.

"Trust me. Just watch." I had more questions than I had answers, but it was clear I was bugging the hell out of him. I continued to watch the insanity on the screen, and I started to get kind of hooked.

Suddenly, I whacked Nathan on the arm. "Hold on.

I thought you said that's her brother!"

"He is," he said with a smirk. His eyes were fixed on me as the scene unfolded.

"Are… are they? No…wait. No. Oh my god, Nooooooo! What in the hell?"

"Told ya," he snickered. The way he looked at me with his mischievous grin and a sparkle in his eye made my heart melt.

"Ewwwwww!" I turned to him with feigned disgust. "You sicko."

He laughed, and suddenly he looked years younger. "This shit is good! Now do what I said and just *watch*."

With a huff, I nestled back in my spot. I could tell he was getting a kick out of my indignant reactions, but I didn't care. I was actually having fun. For the next few minutes, I forced myself to remain silent and hold my questions. The more I watched, the more obsessed I became. There was something about the characters that made me forget everything around me and totally immerse myself in the show. It was a welcome reprieve, and I could see why he liked it. Just when I thought I knew what to expect, there would be a plot twist that would knock me off my feet. I loved it. Now and then I'd sneak a glance at Nathan, only to find that he was already watching me. I had a feeling he was enjoying introducing me to all the depravity. In no time, we'd watched two episodes and were going into our third. Every time the scene became intense or scary, I found myself inching closer to him. I couldn't help myself.

Just being close to him made me feel safe. I knew it was late, and I worried that I might have been keeping him up. "Are you working tomorrow?"

"I'm taking a couple of days off."

I was about to reply when the handsome brother suddenly got his hand chopped off. Floored by what happened, I gasped and sprang out of my seat. I looked at him in horror and noticed the little smirk on his face. I quickly sat down and groaned, "Tell me that didn't just happen."

"Oh yeah, it just happened, and he had it coming."

"But *why*? He needs his hand! He's the king's guard! He's not that bad."

"Oh, he is that bad. He pushed a kid out the window, and that's just the start of it."

I sighed and shook my head. "I'm gonna need a minute to wrap my head around this." Before I had a chance to recover, I was sucked back into the show. I grabbed a blanket from the back of the couch and threw it over my legs and part of his. Mesmerized by the show, I curled into my pillow and enjoyed the escape. My eyelids were heavy as I tried to fight my exhaustion, but I was just too tired. My resistance was futile, and I finally drifted off to sleep.

Chapter 3
Nitro

I hadn't even realized Tristen had fallen asleep until I noticed the questions had completely stopped. Where at first they had been a bit distracting, especially considering there were so many, seeing her get sucked into my favorite show made it worth it. I liked seeing her eyes light up with excitement, her brows furrow with confusion, and her nose crinkle when she saw something grotesque. Everything about her fascinated me, and I just couldn't get enough. Unfortunately, I didn't have the chance. She was sound asleep, completely exhausted from a long day, and despite her interest in the show, she just couldn't hold on any longer. I stood up and lifted her into my arms, cradling her close to my chest as I carried her down the hall to her room. She never woke as I laid her down on the bed and covered her with the blanket I found in a heap on the floor. Reluctantly, I left her and went to my own room to sleep.

We both slept late, and it was well after lunch before either of us got up. I was in the kitchen hunting for something to eat when she walked in. Her hair was wet from the shower, and she was wearing black leggings with a Seattle Seahawks t-shirt. She walked over and sat down at the counter while I continued to rummage for food. "Morning. You hungry?"

"Starving. What do you have?"

"Depends on what you're wanting. I've got nothing…and I've got, um, nothing."

"Surely there's something up there."

"I've got eggs, ramen noodles, bacon, garlic, cheese, and a rotisserie chicken."

She stood up and started towards me. "I think I can work with that. Do you want lunch or breakfast?"

"What? You really think you can come up with something good using all this?"

"Well, sure," she said as she propped her hand on her hip. "So, lunch or breakfast?"

"I'm gonna go with lunch. Show me what you got."

She immediately set to work gathering pots and pans. "Grab the bacon." While she boiled the noodles, she turned on the skillet. I handed the bacon to her and asked "What else you need?"

"Two eggs and some olive oil. And grab that cheese while you're at it."

I leaned back against the counter and watched in awe as she turned my largely unused kitchen into a four-star restaurant. I had a feeling this girl would never stop surprising me. In a matter of minutes, she'd made some kind of pasta that not only looked good, but smelled delicious. I grabbed the drinks, forks, and napkins, while she filled our bowls. My stomach growled as she brought them over to the table.

Looking rather proud she sat down and said,

"Okay, we're all set."

"I've gotta say, I'm impressed."

"Well, you haven't tasted it yet." She watched anxiously as I took a heaping forkful and shoved it in my mouth.

"So? What do you think?"

"Holy shit, this is the bomb," I garbled through my mouthful of food.

"Glad you think so." A light pink blush crossed her face as she took a bite.

"Where'd you learn to cook like this?"

"My parents worked a lot, so Josie and I tried to help out. We were always trying out different combinations. Over time, we figured out what worked together... but we had lots of fails. Lots." She laughed, and I thought I'd never heard a more beautiful sound. "So, did you ever help out in the kitchen growing up?"

A rueful smile crossed my face as I remembered all the times my mother had tried to teach me in the kitchen. "Yeah, you could say that. I bet I had *way* more fails than you though."

"I seriously doubt that. You don't know Josie. That girl would put the most random things together... and some of it was just gross. I swear I had food poisoning at least four times as a kid."

"Ha! That's nothing. I used to trick my brother Colton into eating my concoctions after I'd screwed them up. There was nothing that boy wouldn't eat.... Until he had my 'Potted Meat Pie.' I don't think I've ever seen another human being turn that shade of green. I did it so often that my mother had to ban me from the kitchen *and* the garage."

"The *garage*?" she asked incredulously.

"Hey, I never said what was *in* my meat pies. I got pretty creative during my teenage years," I laughed. As I looked at her smiling, I realized it'd been a long time since I'd had a happy memory of my brother, and it wouldn't have happened if it hadn't been for her.

We bantered back and forth as we finished our Ramen Carbonara, as she dubbed it, and we were about to clear the table when Tristen suddenly said, "Nathan?"

"Yeah?"

"Something's been on my mind and…" She paused for a moment before she continued. "You'd done what Cotton had asked you to do. Why didn't you just leave it at that… Why didn't you just send me back to the club?" Her eyes searched mine as she waited for my reply.

I took a deep breath. "That's not an easy question to answer."

"Try. It's something I need to know."

I paused and considered just how much I wanted her to know. I'd kept her for my own selfish reasons, and I didn't want to drive her away. Trying to keep it simple, I said, "Being in the worst place I could have ever imagined being, I just wanted to get the hell out of there. I thought it would be easy to just get the girl and go… but then I saw you."

"What do you mean?"

I didn't know how to explain how one moment had changed me -- how I had known there was something special about her. Hell, I didn't understand it myself. She'd captivated me in ways I couldn't even comprehend. Knowing I was taking a risk, I laid it all out. "When I looked into your eyes, I saw a quiet strength, a fire burning deep inside, and even through all the drugs, it was still burning bright. It pulled me to you. Seeing you made me forget about the hell I was standing in. It made me forget the danger around us. There was never any choice. I was getting you out of there and getting you safe, even if it meant taking you away from the brothers."

Her eyes never left mine as she let my words sink in. It was a lot. I knew it was, but she deserved to know. A tear trickled down her cheek as she said, "I'd never been so scared in my life. I saw those men and heard the awful things they were saying, but I was frozen with fear and dazed by the drugs. I thought my life as I'd always known it was over. I'd all but given up... until I saw you. I can't explain what was going on in my mind, but I knew when I looked at you, there was hope. There's no way I can ever repay you for saving me and Lauren from that hell."

Trying to make light of our heavy conversation, I said, "You just did. That was one hell of a Ramen Carbonara. We'll call it even." I chuckled as I stood up and carried our dishes to the sink.

When I turned around, I saw her wiping her eyes before she said, "So, what did I miss last night? Any more dismemberment?"

"Oh, you have no idea, woman. Shit got real. Wanna see? I'll restart it."

Chapter 4
Tristen

We spent the next few days just getting to know each other, and I hated that it was coming to an end. I had started to feel like I was seeing the real him, and I couldn't get enough. Unfortunately, Nathan had to go back to work, and it was time for me to start looking for a job. While I was eager to get started, the bed was awfully warm, and I was finding it hard to get up. I finally forced myself to kick the covers off and was about to head to the bathroom for a shower when I tripped, falling flat on my face with a resounding thud.

I was still lying there when I heard an unfamiliar voice shout through the door. "Ms. Carmichael... Is everything okay?"

"Um... yeah." I quickly pulled myself up off the floor. "Everything's fine."

"You sure?" he asked.

"Yep. I'm good." I walked over to the door, eased it open, and found a man wearing a dark navy-blue suit standing in the hallway. The first thing that I noticed about him was his size. He was a big guy, casting a shadow that nearly filled the room, with bulging muscles that seemed to go on for days. His tailored shirt fit him perfectly, and there was no doubt that he spent a lot of time in the gym. He was young, probably in his early thirties, and if it weren't for the smile on his handsome face, I might've found him threatening. "Hey."

"Hi, Ms. Carmichael." He extended his hand out to me. "I'm Max."

I smiled as I shook his hand. "Nice to meet you, Max."

"There's coffee in the kitchen."

"Okay, thanks." I was still a little out of sorts, half asleep and half dazed from my fall, so it took me a second to realize it wasn't Nathan that had come to the door. Wondering where he might be, I asked, "Will Nathan be at breakfast?"

"He already headed out." He motioned towards the kitchen. "But I'll be out front if you need anything."

When he turned to leave, I closed the door and went over to the dresser. I was in desperate need of a hot shower and a change of clothes. It was time for me to do some job hunting, and I needed to get an early start. Once I was dressed, I looked myself over in the mirror and gave my hair and makeup one last check. I'd always loved my blonde hair, but after the kidnapping and knowing it was one of the reasons they'd taken me, I'd decided to dye it dark. While I liked it, it still felt strange to see my new reflection. After one last look, I grabbed my phone and went over to the small desk in the corner of the room. I had several jobs that I wanted to check out. After I made a few calls, I found out that most of the jobs I was interested in were already filled, but I did manage to score an interview at one of the local hot spots. My stomach was turning somersaults as I headed down the hall towards the kitchen. When I walked in, Max was sitting at the table reading the newspaper and eating a bagel. I poured myself a cup of coffee and sat down at the kitchen counter. I grabbed my phone out of my purse and checked my messages and email. Once I was done, I got up and started for the door. "I'll check ya later, Max. Thanks for the coffee."

"Hold up." Max stood up and rushed towards me. "I'll take you wherever you need to go."

"That's okay. I can just get a taxi."

I continued towards the door, until I heard him say, "That's not an option, Ms. Carmichael."

Confused, I whipped around to face him. "What do you mean, that's not an option?"

"If you have somewhere you'd like to go, I'll take you."

"I got that part, Max." I stepped towards him. "What's the problem with me taking a taxi?"

"It's not exactly a problem..." he started.

"Good." I turned and started walking towards the door. "I'll be back later."

"Ms. Carmichael." His voice was stern and a little more forceful than I'd expected. "I can't let you do that."

"First, stop calling me *Ms. Carmichael*. It's freaking me out. And second... I'm not going to ask this again... why can't I take a taxi?"

He let out a deep breath and started for the door. "It's my job. I'm here to make sure you have everything you need. So, why don't you just tell me where you'd like to go, *Tristen*?"

"Something tells me there's more to it, but fine. The first stop is just around the corner at the West End Bar and Grill."

I followed him to the elevator, then out to his black BMW. He opened the back door, and I slipped inside. I should've been happy to have my own personal chauffeur, but I wasn't, not even a little. Instead, I was aggravated and felt like I was being treated like a child. Obviously, Nathan didn't think I could handle doing things on my own, so he sent a stupid babysitter to see after me. Unfortunately for him, I wasn't someone who enjoyed being supervised.

Once he pulled up to the front of the building, I quickly opened the door and hopped out. "I'll be back in a few."

"No rush. I'll be here waiting, unless you'd like me to come inside with you."

The pitch of my voice shot up several octaves as I screeched, "No." I put my purse on my shoulder and stepped up onto the curb. "That won't be necessary."

I shut the car door and headed inside. I walked over to the hostess counter and was greeted by a blonde in her mid-thirties wearing a black halter top and short, black miniskirt. She leaned forward as she rested her elbows on the counter and smiled. "Hey, doll. What can

I do for you?"

"Hi, I'm Tristen Carmichael." I'd done my research on the West End Bar and Grill, and it was one of the new hot spots in the area. In one night's time, they served between two to three hundred people, and their lunch crowd was equally as busy. I needed good tips, which meant I needed as many customers as I could get. I hoped that West End would help get me a good start. "Is Mr. Marino here?"

Her smile quickly disappeared as her eyes roamed over me. Once she was done sizing me up, a disapproving snarl crossed her face letting me know she didn't approve of my black V-neck shirt and jeans combination. "You here for the waitress job?"

"I was told the opening was for a bartender position."

"That's if you make the cut. You'll waitress first. If that works out, then you'll move up to 'tender." She flipped her hair over her shoulder as she looked behind her. "Hey, Tony! She's here."

"Send her on back!" a man shouted from behind the bar. It was still early, so the lunch crowd hadn't shown up. In a half hour, the place would be buzzing with people and doing an interview at the bar would be damn near impossible.

She looked back over to me like she'd smelled something bad and said, "He's over at the bar."

"Yeah, I caught that." I walked past the counter and over to the bar, and I was surprised to find a young Joey from *Friends* standing there waiting for me. Well, it wasn't the actual Joey, but he looked just like him. "Hi, Mr. Marino. I'm Tristen Carmichael. We spoke earlier about the bartender position."

"Yeah. Yeah, I remember." He smiled and offered me his hand, shaking it firmly. "Have a seat."

I reached in my bag and pulled out my résumé. "I emailed you a copy, but I thought I'd bring an extra one just in case."

He took it from my hand and glanced over it. "So, you're interested in the bartender position?"

"I am."

"Well, it doesn't look like you've got much experience with it."

"No, but I'm a fast learner." I could tell he wasn't buying it, so I took a deep breath and pushed a little harder. "It may not show it on paper, but I do have a lot of experience, Mr. Marino. I've worked hard and learned a lot over the past couple of years. I'm dependable, trustworthy, and I'm always on time. I know how to deal with a rough crowd, and the not-so-rough crowd. Whatever you've got, I can handle it. I just need the chance to prove it."

He smiled, and I knew I'd won him over. "I tell you what… we'll start you off as an assistant. You'll help out around the bar and that will give you a chance to pick up on a few things. Tips will be shared sixty- forty, and we'll work out your hours from week to week."

"That sounds great."

"Good. I'll let the boss know we've got ourselves a new bartender."

I stood up and smiled. "So, when do I start?"

"Be here at ten tomorrow morning. I'll get you a uniform from the back."

"I'll be here. Thanks, Mr. Marino."

"Don't thank me yet." He laughed as he motioned to the girl up front. "You'll have to work with our girl, Brooklyn."

"Oh, I'm sure we'll manage just fine." I started walking towards the front door and as I passed the hostess counter, I looked over my shoulder at Brooklyn. "See you tomorrow."

She rolled her eyes and gave me an unenthusiastic wave goodbye. I was just about to walk out the front door when I spotted Max's black BMW sitting out front. I stopped in my tracks and quickly turned around. "Hey, is there a back door I could use?"

Brooklyn looked at me like I was crazy as she pointed towards the service entrance. "You can go through the kitchen."

"Thanks!"

I don't know what I was thinking. I certainly wasn't thinking of Max or his job as I hurried through the kitchen, swerving past the cooks with their pots and pans or the bus boys with the dish buckets. I only had one thing on my mind. Me. I had things I wanted to take care of, and I didn't want Hawkeye watching my every move. So, I did the only thing I could—I ditched him.

Chapter 5
Nitro

It'd only been a few weeks, but it seemed like a lifetime since I'd stepped foot in the office. I knew Murray was taking care of things, but it just wasn't the same. The business was important to me. It was my father's legacy, and from the day I'd taken the reins, I'd been determined to make it a success. To make that happen, I'd always made sure I knew firsthand what was going on—especially when it came to getting in our shipments. The stakes were high, and there was no room for mistakes—period. Like me, the men we dealt with didn't do excuses. They had people counting on them, and their lives were on the line if they didn't deliver. It was a risk, a serious risk, but when the delivery was successful and all parties were satisfied, it could be a very profitable business. It was up to me to make sure that everything went as planned and no detail was overlooked.

Staying off the radar was one of most important parts of our business. To ensure our safety, we had several warehouses in the main cargo dock in Port Angeles, along with several others hidden inland. They were tucked away, deep in the mountains for added security when things got heated. The risk of getting caught was growing by the day. It was just part of the game. Over the years, I'd learned a few tricks of the trade, like using the rotation method for storing our goods and frequently changing up delivery locations. By swapping things up from month to month, it made it difficult for the cops to track us, and it kept our competitors from trying to fuck with our cargo. We also had several shell companies—a full-service log yard along with a couple of nightclubs and bars—to help launder the influx of funds arriving each month. I chose the log yard in Port Angeles so we'd have access to the dock and incoming freight. It was a pain in the ass, but logging was fairly profitable, and it gave us an easy way to smuggle in our goods. I knew nothing about logging, but thankfully, I had Bennett to handle things there at the yard. He was young, but he'd grown up in the business and knew everything there was to know about making a logging yard successful. I hadn't had much contact with him while I was gone, so I decided to stop in and check on him before I went to the office.

When I walked up, Bennett was talking to one of our delivery guys, and it was clear that he was pissed. His shoulders were drawn back and his face was growing redder by the minute. By the time they were done talking, Bennett looked like he was ready to blow. "What the hell was that all about?"

"Stupid motherfucker tried to pawn off a load of second rate timber at the regular charge."

"And?"

"It's not gonna fucking happen." He looked back

over to the dock. "I told him if he dropped the price by seventy-five percent we'd consider taking it."

"You sure that's a good idea? You gonna be able to unload it?"

"Don't you worry about that, boss," he boasted. "You know I can sell a fucking popsicle to an Eskimo. It just helps to have the right price."

"You got a time on our next shipment?"

"I just talked to Ryder. He said he'd have it here before two."

Ryder was one of my best. He was a big guy, six-four and built for knocking heads, and he never failed to bring in the shipments on time. Knowing they had it covered, I turned and started walking towards the parking lot. "I'm headed over to the office. Let me know when he gets here."

"You got it, boss. Good to have you back."

"Good to be back."

I got in my SUV and headed over to our main warehouse. Things were relatively quiet when I walked in. Most of the guys didn't come in until later in the morning, which meant I had about a couple of hours to work without any distractions, or so I thought. I hadn't been working long when the door flew open and Murray finally came strolling in. With a big, shit-eating grin, he sat down on the edge of my desk and crossed his arms. "Well, well, well. Look who the cat dragged in."

Completely ignoring his jab at my absence, I asked, "Any word from Dez?"

"Not wasting any time, huh?" he teased. "Talked with him last night. Everything is set for tomorrow night. I told you I would handle it."

"Good."

He stood up and walked over to his desk. Once he sat down, he looked over to me with a puzzled look. "You wanna tell me why you put a hold on Cotton's next shipment?"

"Nope."

"Is it a temporary thing?"

"Nope."

"So, we're done with them?"

"Yep."

"Mm hm. So, does this break from the club have something to do with your little trip to Arizona?" When I didn't answer, he kept pushing. "Seriously? You're not going to say something here?"

"There's nothing to say."

"It's not like you to go running off like that, so I'm guessing it had something to do with a girl."

"None of that matters." I gave him a warning glare. "I'm back now."

"Good. I hope that means you've got your head in the game. We have a lot of stock to unload in the next couple of days."

"Whether I'm here or not, my head is always in the game."

For the next hour, I was actually able to work in peace. I was finally making progress, but I was interrupted when my burner cell rang. I took it from my back pocket and answered. "Yeah?"

There was a brief hesitation before I heard him say, "Got a problem."

"I'm gonna need more than that."

"It's Ms. Carmichael." He paused before he continued. "She gave me the slip."

I stood up and squeezed the phone tightly in my hand. "How the fuck did that happen?"

"She went into the West End bar for her job interview with Tony. She went in the front door, but she went out the back without me knowing it."

"Fuck!"

"I've gotta tell ya, boss... She wasn't exactly happy that I was driving her. She was pretty fired up. I figure that's why she bolted."

"I don't give a fuck why she bolted! It's your job to watch over her. Period!" I roared. "Find her!"

"I'm on it."

"I want to know the minute you find her." I slammed the phone down on my desk with an aggravated growl. "Dammit!"

Murray shook his head as he muttered under his breath, "Yeah... he's definitely a man with his head in the game."

"Fuck off, Murray."

"I'm glad to know I haven't lost my touch." He smiled wide. "I was right about the girl."

"Don't you have some work to do?" I growled as I

tried to focus on my computer screen. Thankfully, I had plenty of work to keep my mind off Tristen. I thought it would help distract me from the fact that she'd gone AWOL, but it didn't. I tried making a few calls and sorting through all my messages, but nothing helped. I looked down at my watch and cursed myself when I saw that it'd only been fifteen minutes since I'd gotten off the phone with Max. I was growing impatient. I reached for my phone to send him a message, but he'd beaten me to it.

Max:

Found her.

Me:

Where?

Max:

Tracked her phone. She's at the college.

Me:

Doing what?

Max:

Don't know, but I'm about to find out.

Me:

Good.

Damaged Goods

Max:

You want me to pick her up?

Me:

No

Me:

Make sure she knows you're there.

Max:

You sure about that?

Me:

Absolutely.

I'd asked Max to watch her for a reason. In our line of business, you could never be too careful. He was there to keep her safe, and he was going to do his job whether she liked it or not. Period. It had only been a few seconds when I got another message from him.

Max:

She's at the enrollment office.

I remembered her telling me that she wanted to go to college, but I thought she'd meant later, much later. Regardless, I knew she was safe and that was all that mattered. As ordered, Max continued to give me updates every hour or so, letting me know exactly where she was and what she was doing. It might've been a little over the top, but it gave me peace of mind to know she was okay.

It was well after dark by the time I got back to the condo, and I was already on edge from a shitty day. Finding Max waiting for me when I got off the elevator didn't help things. Over the years, he'd more than proven that he was reliable--- it was why I'd hired him—but he'd fucked up, and he knew it. I was in no mood to talk, so I told him, "We'll discuss it later."

"Understood." He started towards the elevator, but he hesitated. "Today was on me, one hundred percent. It won't happen again."

He should've left it, but the door had been opened and there was no going back. As I took a step towards him, I could feel the muscles in my neck tighten. "You're damn right it's on you, Max!"

"I know I screwed up, but I thought she'd accepted the fact that I was there for her. I had no way of knowing she'd run out on me."

"It's your fucking job to know."

"There's no excuse, boss. I know I screwed up. You have my word it won't happen again."

"It had damn well better not, or it will be more than just your job on the line."

I'd said enough. I was ready for the day to be over, so I started for the door. I was about to go inside when he said, "You do realize she gave me the slip for a reason."

It wasn't exactly the smartest thing he could have said when I was already pissed, but he said it nonetheless. I turned and glared at him. "It doesn't fucking matter."

"It mattered to *her*."

"Fuck off, Max. That's enough of your bullshit."

He turned and started to leave. As he got on the elevator, he looked at me with his eyebrow cocked high. "You just hate it when I'm right."

The doors shut before I had a chance to respond, leaving me even more frustrated than before. I stormed into the condo and found Tristen on the sofa watching TV. I wasn't greeted with one of her bright smiles or 'How was your day?'. Hell, she didn't even turn around. She had a point to make, and she was making damn well sure she made it. I'd met my quota on arguments for the day, so I kept walking, leaving her there to stew in her own anger. I should've stopped and talked to her or tried to work out this thing between us, but I just didn't have it in me.

I walked into my room and slammed the door. Without turning on the lights, I laid down on the bed. I was exhausted. My crappy day had taken its toll, and I just wanted to sleep it off. I closed my eyes, but I soon became restless as all the craziness of the day came crashing through my mind. I was thinking about Joe and that damn load of timber when I finally drifted off. I had no idea how long I'd been asleep when I was awakened by a blood-curdling scream. At first I thought it was just my imagination, that I was having one of my dreams, but then I heard it for the second time. I rushed out of bed and headed down the hall to Tristen's room. I paused at the door, listening for any kind of struggle, and that was when I realized she was having a nightmare.

"No, no, no... please don't," she begged.

I reached for the door knob and was relieved to find it unlocked. I slowly eased it open and found Tristen thrashing around on the bed. Tears were streaming down her face as she mumbled incoherent phrases under her breath. Trying my best not to spook her, I lowered myself onto the bed and gently pulled her into my arms, cradling her close to my chest. Hearing her little whimpers and cries made my chest grow tight, and I wanted nothing more than to make them stop. I lowered my mouth to her ear and whispered, "I'm right here, Angel."

I repeated it over and over again until she started to settle down. With her head resting on my shoulder, she curled into my side. Just seeing her looking so peaceful, so angelic, made my day from hell all but disappear. There was no denying that I felt something for her. Hell, the pull to her was so strong she could've been at the end of the Earth, and I still would've felt it. I couldn't explain it, but I liked it. I'd always hated the feeling that I was missing something, that I'd left something behind. When I was with her, I didn't feel that. Instead, I felt peace. As much as I liked having her next to me and feeling the warmth of her body next to mine, though, I had to move. Every second I stayed in that spot, it became more and more difficult to stay awake. Knowing she needed her rest, I slowly slid my way over to the edge of the bed and was just about to lower her to the pillows when I caught her looking up at me.

"Please don't go." I tried to resist, but it was no use. She was just too beautiful, too fucking tempting, and I knew there was no way in hell I was ever going to be able to tell her no.

I nodded as I eased back into my spot. "I didn't realize you were awake."

"I haven't been for long." She laid her head back on my shoulder as she released a deep breath. "I thought they were getting better."

"The nightmares?" She nodded against my chest. "They will in time. For now, just try to get some rest. I'll stay here until you fall back asleep."

"Thank you," she answered in barely a whisper.

When her breathing became slow and deep and her body completely still, I knew she was sleeping soundly. I carefully lowered her onto the pillows and lifted myself out of the bed. I stood over her for several moments to make sure that she hadn't woken up when I'd moved her. Once I knew for sure that she was okay, I went back to my room and got into the bed. I tried to go back to sleep, but it was impossible to ignore the coldness I felt without her next to me or the faint scent of her perfume on my t-shirt. It'd been a lifetime since

I'd had any real reaction to a woman. Sure, I'd had sex with women, lots and lots of sex, but there was never anything more. I'd figured I was broken and incapable of feeling... until her. I couldn't help but wonder if maybe, just maybe, she'd be the one person that could save me from myself.

Chapter 6
Tristen

My dreams used to be filled with hope and possibilities, a sneak peek into a desperately wanted future, but those kinds of dreams no longer came. Now whenever I closed my eyes, I was back in that room. I felt the chain gripping my wrist, the sweat trickling down my spine, and the all-consuming fear that took over my every thought each time I heard their footsteps coming down the hall. I always knew what was coming—the needle. At first, I'd tried to resist them, twisting and pulling against their grip, but it had only made it worse. They'd known how to cause pain without leaving marks: twisting a handful of my hair in their fist, forcing my arm behind my back, or delivering a painful jab to my abdomen. Eventually, I'd stopped trying to fight and let them shoot the drugs into my veins. It was absolute hell, and there was no escape, not even in my dreams. I tried to wake myself up. I tried to break the cycle, but I was trapped. I couldn't pull myself out of the nightmare. Then, I heard his voice. It was soft and low, just barely a whisper, but it was enough. The dingy, old room with the putrid yellow walls and the dirty mattress started to fade. The overwhelming panic subsided, and I was finally able to let go of the fear. For the first time in weeks, I felt safe—I *was* safe, and it was all because of him.

The next morning, I pulled myself out of bed and rushed to the bathroom to take a shower. I was eager to start my first day of work. I turned on my shower and was about to undress when I caught a glimpse of myself in the mirror. I was surprised to see a goofy little grin on my face. It'd been a long time since I'd had a reason to smile, but thinking of Nathan holding me in his arms until I was able to go back to sleep definitely gave me something to smile about. I was still grinning like the Cheshire Cat even after I'd gotten dressed and headed to the kitchen for a cup of coffee. Unfortunately, that giddy little feeling died a miserable death when I found Max sitting at the table.

He had to be furious with me. I'd heard Nathan arguing with him the night before, and I had no doubt that had only made him even more angry. I bit my bottom lip as I headed over to the counter and reached for the coffee pot. I almost dropped it when I heard him say, "Good morning, Ms. Carmichael."

"Good morning, Max." After I poured my coffee, I walked over to the table and sat down next to him. He looked up at me with a half-smile, and I knew I had to do it. "I wanted to tell you that I'm sorry about yesterday."

"Okay."

"Well... maybe I should clarify that a bit. I'm sorry that you got chewed out by Nathan, but I'm not sorry that I ran off without you."

"Glad we got that cleared up," he grumbled under his breath as he took a sip of his coffee.

"I really am sorry. I didn't mean to cause you trouble, but the whole thing rubbed me the wrong way. Nathan never mentioned to me that he was going to have someone watching over me, otherwise I would've sorted it out with him."

"I'm sure he figured you were used to it."

"What does that mean?"

He leaned forward and studied my reaction as he asked, "You were one of the Satan's Fury girls, right?"

"Not exactly." I knew where he was going, and I tried to swallow my annoyance. "I worked there."

"Okay. So, you worked there. However you want to say it, you were part of the club. When they ran into trouble or your safety was a concern, they had someone watching over you."

"But that was different."

"How?"

"The club was under attack… people were after them for one reason or another. They put us on lockdown or whatever because they didn't want anything to happen to us."

"It's the same."

"It's not the same. Nathan doesn't have people coming after him."

"That's not exactly true."

"What are you talking about?"

"It's not for me to explain, but I can tell you this:

your safety is important to him, and it's my job to make sure nothing happens to you. I plan to do my job and to do it well, whether you're on board or not."

"Why is he so concerned about my safety?"

"You'll have to talk to him about that."

I groaned as I rested my forehead down onto the table. "He isn't exactly the easiest guy to talk to."

"You have no idea."

I looked up at him with my eyebrow raised. "Gee, thanks."

"I'm just telling you the way it is." He leaned back in his chair and crossed his arms. "There are things you'll have to get used to."

"Fine." My mind was spinning, and I just wanted it to stop. It was my first day at work, and I wanted to get on with it. I stood up and put my empty coffee cup in the sink. "I need to get to work."

His lips curled into a mischievous grin as he snickered, "Ready when you are."

"Of course you are," I groaned.

Since I was in training, I knew I would be busy, especially in a place like West End. From the minute they opened their doors, the crowds steadily rolled in, and I was excited to have the chance to work there. More customers meant more tips, but it was more than that. I had money—plenty of money—but I hadn't earned it. It was my parents' money, the money they'd spent their entire lives working for, but I didn't feel like I deserved to have it. My sister, Josie, had done the responsible thing by going off to college and preparing for her future, while I'd acted like a spoiled brat and run away from home. I'd made so many mistakes, but I refused to keep living in the past. One way or another, I was going to find a way to make them proud of me, and while I was at it, I'd find a way to make *me* proud of me.

Once I'd gotten my things, I headed back to the kitchen to find Max. "I'm ready."

He nodded, and I followed him down to the car. He opened the door, and I slid inside. Seconds later, we were on our way to the bar. "How long is your shift?"

"He didn't say."

He reached into his front pocket and then extended his hand into the backseat. "Here's my card. Just call or text when you're ready for me to come pick you up."

"You aren't staying?"

He looked at me in the rearview mirror. "You'll be safe here."

"Okay." I stepped out of the car and headed inside. I turned back towards the car and gave him a quick wave.

He waited for me to go in before he drove off. I was a bundle of nerves as I walked into the bar. Brooklyn was standing at the hostess counter with two of the other waitresses. One of them was blonde like her, but her hair seemed more natural and less processed than Brooklyn's. The other waitress was tall with naturally wavy, brown hair and big, brown eyes that reminded me of one of my sister's old China dolls. When Brooklyn saw me heading in their direction, she rolled her eyes and sneered, "She's Katie's replacement."

I lifted my hand and gave them a half-wave as I smiled. "Hi. I'm Tristen."

"Hey, girl. I'm Ava." The curvy brunette smiled as she took a step towards me. "Come on."

"Thanks, Ava."

We'd only taken a few steps when Brooklyn shouted, "She's yours for the day, Ava. If she screws up, it's on you."

"I've got it," she shouted back. It was clear that she wasn't Brooklyn's biggest fan when she grumbled under her breath, "Fuckwad."

When we got back to the staff room, Ava gathered up my uniform and showed me where to change. "Thanks for your help, Ava."

"No problem." She turned and started walking towards the door. "I'll meet you out front by the kitchen."

"I'll be right there."

Once I was done, I headed out to meet Ava. She motioned for me to do a full turn, then said, "Looking good."

"You don't think the skirt is too short?"

"Hell, no. Not with your figure. With legs like that, the shorter the better." She handed me a note pad and started walking. "Today, you'll be my shadow. It's your chance to ask questions and learn what you need to know." She looked back up front to where Brooklyn was still talking to the other blonde. "But tomorrow you'll be on your own. Jada is off for the next couple of days, so Tony will want you serving. I hope you're a fast learner."

"I am."

"Good. Now, let's get to it."

The next few hours were a complete blur. People just kept rolling in, and poor Ava never stopped moving. She was buzzing around from the kitchen to the tables to the bar and back again, and I started to worry that I'd never be able to keep up. She seemed to notice that I was getting a little panicked, so she stopped for a second to reassure me. "I know it's a lot to take in, but it really isn't all that bad. It's all about timing. Once you catch on, you'll be fine. You'll see."

"How long have you worked here?"

"A couple of months."

I swallowed hard, trying to push down my anxiety, and smiled. "OK. Let's do this."

Things slowed down after the lunch crowd left, so Ava suggested that we take a quick lunch break. She grabbed us a couple of sandwiches, and since it was a nice day outside, we headed out to the front deck. As soon as she sat down, she smiled. "You're doing great, by the way."

"I'm not so sure, but thanks. I think I'm getting the hang of it."

"You'll do fine." She took a bite of her sandwich

and looked over at me, studying me as she chewed. "So, what's your deal?"

"My deal?"

"You know… where ya from and all that."

I hesitated for a moment. I wasn't quite ready to tell the world about my fiasco with the cartel or how Nathan rescued me, so I avoided it all together. "Well, there's not much to tell."

"Somehow I doubt that." She took a sip of her sweet tea and continued, "A chick like you definitely has a story."

"I guess you could say that I'm a girl who's made some stupid mistakes and is looking for a fresh start."

"Hmm… sounds like some asshole did a real number on you."

I nodded. "You could say that."

Before she could respond, Tony stuck his head out the side door and yelled, "A big group just came in. We need you two out front."

"We'll be right there."

By the time we got back inside, Brooklyn had already seated a large group of men in Ava's section. Before we walked over to the table, Ava looked at me worriedly. "I'm gonna need your help with this one."

"You've got it."

We spent the next hour serving the group, making sure they had everything they needed. By the time they were gone, I was feeling much better about things. I'd caught on to the timing and had gotten into the groove. I even caught Brooklyn watching us from time to time, and I think she was surprised by how well I was doing. The dinner crowd came and went, and at the end of my shift I felt pretty confident. Once we got everything cleaned up for the night, I went to the back room to change and text Max. I was completely exhausted, so I didn't waste any time. I grabbed my things and headed out front. I hadn't made it far when Tony stopped me.

"Hey, how was the first day?"

"I think it went okay."

"Ava said you did great. You think you can handle a few tables of your own tomorrow?"

"Sure."

"Good to hear. I'll see you in the morning."

As expected, Max was waiting for me by the front door. As soon as I got inside the car, I leaned my head back against the headrest and closed my eyes. He was quiet on the way back to the condo, so I assumed his day was like mine—long and exhausting. When we got off the elevator, he smiled and said, "See you in the morning."

"Thanks, Max."

He waited as I opened the door and stepped inside. I was surprised to find that the lights were out and there was no sign of Nathan. I figured he'd gone to sleep, so I decided to do the same. As I got in the shower, I thought back on my day and was rather pleased with myself. I'd survived my first day and actually enjoyed it. With a smile plastered on my face, I changed into my pajamas and crawled into bed. I'd forgotten what it was like to be so happy, and I owed it all to Nathan. I turned to face my door, and before I realized what I was doing, I got out of the bed and started towards Nathan's room. For reasons I didn't understand myself, I wanted to share my day with him. I stopped at his door and raised my hand to knock, but as I stood there staring at his door doubt washed over me. It was late, he was probably sleeping, and he didn't want to hear about my silly waitressing job. Feeling foolish, I turned and rushed back to my room. I'd just crawled back into bed, when I heard a tap at my door. Damn.

"It's open." My heart started to race as I watched the door slowly creak open and Nathan stepped inside. His hair was disheveled like he'd been sleeping, and he was wearing black pajama pants with nothing else. Holy hell. I'm pretty sure my entire body melted right there on the spot. I tried to fight it, but a little gasp escaped my lips as my eyes roamed over the muscles of his bare chest. I couldn't have dreamed up a sexier image.

"You okay?" His voice was low and husky, sending little chills down my spine.

"Yeah. I'm fine." I pulled myself up and turned to face him as I propped myself up on my elbow. "Did I wake you?"

"No."

He walked over and sat down on the edge of the bed. When he didn't say anything, I started to get nervous and began to babble. "I started my new waitressing job today. It's down at the West End Bar and Grill. It's a really great place, and I really like the people there. Especially Ava. I really like her. She was really sweet and showed me the ropes. I think it'll be a really great job."

"Really?" he teased.

"Yeah, I *really* do." I giggled. "Sorry. I got a little excited there for a minute. It's just so different from working at the clubhouse with all the brothers." His eyebrows furrowed at the mention of the club. It was clear there were hard feelings there, even though I didn't fully understand why. I didn't like to see that look on his face, so I looked away as I explained, "I think it will be a good place to work."

"So, how was it different?"

I told him about everything, from Ava showing me the ropes to serving our big group. He listened and asked questions, and while I was talking, he leaned back on his elbow and rested his head in his hand. It was easy and comfortable being with him, like we'd done it a hundred times before. I continued to rattle on, and the more I talked, the heavier his eyelids became and the lower his head drifted down on the mattress. I wasn't ready for him to go, so I continued to talk about nonsense things, like my new nail polish color and the sandwich I had for lunch. As expected, it didn't take long for him to fall fast asleep. I lay there looking at him, noticing how relaxed and peaceful he looked. Mr. Tough and Powerful was gone, leaving a completely different man who looked young and vulnerable lying next to me. Seeing him that way twisted my heart into knots. It was then that I knew I was in trouble. I just didn't realize how much trouble I was really in.

Chapter 7
Nitro

There are some days a man wakes up knowing it's going to be a shitty day. I'm not sure how. Maybe it was the way he slept, or an unsettling feeling in his bones. Either way, he'd know something was going to go wrong, and he'd spend the entire day trying to prevent it from happening. Today was *not* one of those days for me. For the first time in months, I woke up feeling a little lighter, like the world wasn't weighing down on my shoulders, and I had no doubt that feeling had everything to do with Tristen. She had a way of making the day brighter just by having her near. Over the past couple of days, I hadn't seen much of her and it had begun to get to me, but that was all about to change.

As soon as I found out she had the day off, I canceled my meetings and told Murray I wouldn't be coming in to the office. He gave me all kinds of grief about it, bitching that we were too busy for me to be goofing off, but he was full of shit. I knew the real reason he was complaining, but since I wasn't in the mood to discuss my private life with him, I let him give me hell. It was just easier than talking it out, and besides, I knew he and Max could take care of things for the day. So, I took a hot shower and headed into the kitchen to make breakfast.

I'd just put on a fresh pot of coffee and started the bacon when she walked in. She was wearing an old blue and white t-shirt, and her hair was on top of her head in a messy, tangled bun. She was still rubbing the sleep from her eyes when she sat down at the counter. Without looking up, she grumbled, "Coffee."

I poured her a cup and asked, "Sugar or cream."

Her eyes jerked up to me as her mouth dropped open in surprise. "What are you doing here? Where's Max?"

"Nice to see you, too."

I turned back to the stove as she stammered, "No. Wait. That came out wrong. I... uh... I just wasn't expecting to see you. You're usually gone by the time I get up."

I poured the eggs into the skillet and gave them a quick stir. "Yeah, I know. I decided to take the day off."

"Oh." I looked over my shoulder and caught her quickly reining in her wild hair. She had no idea how beautiful she looked. I wanted to stop her, to tell her that I liked her hair just the way it was, but I was too late. She'd already fixed it. "What's for breakfast?"

"Bacon, eggs, and toast."

"Mmm, that sounds good." She got up and walked over to me. As she peeked over my shoulder, she asked, "Do you need any help?"

"You could grab the bread out of the pantry."

"Sure." She opened the door and leaned in, exposing her long, slender legs, and I had to curse my cock when he stirred beneath my boxers. There was no doubt that he wanted her just as badly as I did. My need to possess her burned deep inside me, and with every second that passed, the flame grew stronger and more intense. There was only one way to keep it under control, and that was Tristen, the very person who set me on fire. Unfortunately, though, my cock and I had to wait. The time wasn't right, but soon, very soon, she would be mine in every way.

She walked back over to me with two different loaves of bread. "White or wheat?"

"You pick. I'm good with either."

"White it is." She smiled as she sauntered over to the counter and pulled out several slices of bread. Once she was done, she took the remaining bread and put it back in the pantry. "Where's the toaster?"

"Top left cabinet."

She opened the cabinet door, and I watched with fascination as her shirt lifted over her hips and revealed her perfect ass. When I noticed her pink lace panties, I groaned beneath my breath. "Fuck."

She placed the toaster on the counter and looked at me with concern. "Everything okay?"

"Yep. All good," I replied as I cleared my throat. Trying my best to redirect my focus, I finished frying the bacon and eggs. When the toast was done, we took everything over to the table and sat down.

After she'd eaten a few bites and drank some of her coffee, she looked over to me and smiled. "It's really good. Thanks for doing all this."

"You helped."

"I don't think I can take much credit. I was still half-asleep when I made the toast."

After I finished eating, I downed the rest of my cup of coffee and carried my dishes over to the sink. "So, you up for an outing today?"

"Sure," she said excitedly. "What do you have in mind?"

"I thought we might take a drive out to the Cape. Maybe we can have a late lunch at a little seafood place I know."

"That sounds perfect." She cleared her spot and hurried towards her room. "I just need to take a quick shower."

"No rush."

A half an hour later, she walked into the kitchen sporting a navy-blue shirt with the shoulders cut out and a pair of old, ripped jeans with boots. Her hair was still damp from the shower, wavy and down around her shoulders, and she had a big smile on her face.

"All set." We were on our way to the car when she turned to me and asked, "While we're out, can we run into town for a few minutes? There's a little shop Ava told me about, and I'd really like to check it out."

"Absolutely."

With the windows down, we headed to the bay and up to Cape Flattery Road. After another half hour of driving, we made it to the trail. It was one of my favorite spots in the area. Once I'd parked the SUV, I turned to Tristen. "You up for a short walk?"

"Absolutely."

After a mile hike, we made our way up to one of the observation decks. It gave us a great view of the Pacific Ocean and all the cliffs and rocks. Standing there next to her as we looked out at the ocean took my breath away, but not because of the blue sky or the waves crashing along the rocks. While they were beautiful, they didn't get to me the way she did. Her smile, the wind blowing through her dark hair, and those incredible blue eyes secretly glancing in my direction affected me in a way I didn't expect. I watched as she followed the peak down to the water. She was just about to put her feet in the water when I felt my phone buzzing in my back pocket.

When I saw who was calling I quickly answered, "Hello."

"Hey, there. I just thought I'd check in. Are you doing okay?"

"I'm doing just fine."

"Did you do that thing I asked you to do for me?"

"Not yet, but I will."

"It will take them some time to get it together, so don't wait too long."

"I know. I told you I'd take care of it."

"I know… I was just making sure." Her voice was soft and low, letting me know she was having one of those days. "You know I'd go with you, but my leg has been giving me some trouble."

I knew her real reason for having me do it myself, and, as much as I hated it, I would do it for her. "I know. I've got it."

"And you'll come to lunch after? Colton is coming."

"What time?"

"Let's say around twelve."

"I'll be there." I assured her.

"Good. I'll see you then." The wind was picking up, along with the voices behind me. There was no doubt she heard the commotion. "I'll let you get back to whatever you were doing."

"Okay, Mom. I'll see you in a couple of days."

"Bye, sweetheart."

I shoved my phone in my back pocket and started down the cliff to meet up with Tristen. When I got down by the water, I found her talking with a young girl who couldn't have been more than three years old. They were looking at a school of fish that were swimming close to the edge of the rocks. "There's bunches of them!"

"Pretty," the little girl exclaimed as she quickly turned to find her mother. "Look, Momma! Fishies!"

Tristen took a step back to give the girl's mother some room to see and smiled at them. I walked up behind her and placed my hand on her waist. "Hey."

She pointed down at the fish excitedly. "Did you see? There's hundreds of them."

"I saw."

"If you put your feet in the water, they'll nibble on your toes," she laughed.

"I'll pass," I replied with a grin.

When the crowds started rolling in, we followed the trail back to the SUV. I walked her over to open her door, and without thinking, I reached for her. I placed my hands along her jaw and pulled her towards me. Then, I gently pressed my lips against hers. I hadn't imagined how soft or how perfect they'd feel pressed up against my own. They were absolute perfection. My hand rested just below her ear, and my thumb caressed her cheek as our breaths mingled. I could feel the beating of her heart against my chest as I pulled her closer. She moaned against my lips as I delved deeper into her mouth, relishing her taste and her warmth. I was lost in her touch, like a man under a spell, and for a brief moment everything around us stilled. Unfortunately, the moment didn't last long. A car door slammed, and our attention was drawn to the voices behind us. I gave her a gentle kiss on her forehead, then opened the door for her to slide inside. Once I'd gotten in, I started the engine and headed out to the main road. I hadn't been driving long when we came upon the Seafood Shack. I looked over to find her gazing out the window, a little smile playing on her beautiful lips. "You ready for a bite to eat?"

"Absolutely."

After I parked, she hopped out and headed for the

front door. There wasn't much to the restaurant. It was just a small place with a couple of booths inside and picnic tables outside, but the food was good and the view was even better. I followed her to the outside patio and over to one of the corner picnic tables. As she looked over the menu she asked, "What's good here?"

"Everything."

Tristen was still mulling it over when Dottie came over to our table. "Hey there, Nate. What can I get you?"

"The usual."

"And you, sweetheart?"

"I'll have the shrimp basket with a glass of lemonade."

Dottie jotted the order down on her notepad as she replied, "Sure thing, hun."

She headed inside and seconds later returned with our drinks. After placing them on the table, she looked over to me and smiled. "I got your orders in."

"Thanks, Dottie."

Murray had discovered the Shack years ago, and since then it had become one of my favorite places, partly because of Dottie. She never failed to treat me like one of her own. "Where's Murray?"

"He's at the office."

"Well, that's too bad. It's a beautiful day."

"That it is." I leaned towards her and smiled. "I'm sure he'll be by soon. You know how he loves your key lime pie."

"Be sure to tell him I asked about him. I'll go check on your order."

"Thanks, Dottie."

It wasn't long before she brought our food out. Tristen's shrimp were in a small tin bucket, while my oysters came on a huge platter that seemed to fill up half the table. "Hope you two are hungry!"

"Starving," Tristen smiled.

We spent the next hour and a half eating and talking. Tristen talked about her childhood with Josie, sharing funny stories about all the things they had gotten into, and I could tell talking about her sister had made her a little homesick. While they'd talked, she hadn't seen Josie since the day we'd left the clubhouse. Tristen had called several times checking on Lauren and just to talk. I knew she was missing her sister. I planned to rectify that, but for the moment, we needed to go. I stood up and said, "I guess we'd better get going."

When we got back to town, I took Tristen over to the second-hand store Ava had told her about. I didn't get what the fuss was all about, but Tristen seemed excited to check it out. We'd been walking around for a few minutes when I noticed Tristen staring at a picture on the wall. When I stepped closer, I saw that it was an image of a couple on a bridge in Paris. They were standing under a red umbrella in the rain. The guy had his arm wrapped around the chick's waist and was holding her close to his side.

"What do you think?"

"It's okay."

"Don't you love how the light reflects off the pavement? And how he's giving her more of the umbrella, so she doesn't get wet?"

I hadn't noticed, but I nodded nonetheless.

"I think I'm going to buy it." She stepped closer and checked the price. "Can I put it in your backseat or in the trunk?"

"Sure."

She rushed over to the counter and gave the lady her credit card. After she finished checking out, the lady came over and took the picture down from the wall. Wearing a huge grin on her face, Tristen took it and headed over to me. "Got it."

"Good deal." I was about to take it from her when I noticed her looking down at the painting thoughtfully. Her eyes seemed to focus on every detail.

"They look so in love."

"Umm," I grumbled.

With a perplexed look on her face, her eyes darted up to mine. "What?"

"Nothing."

"Oh, *that* was definitely *something*."

"I'm just not one to buy in to all that."

"What does that mean *all that*?"

"I'm all for having a good time, enjoying life and everything, but I don't do love, Tristen. All that 'love is patient, love is kind' stuff—it's all bullshit. It only sets you up for heartache and disappointment. I just don't see the point."

I immediately regretted being so candid. Her eyes searched mine as her brow furrowed, and her mouth set into a firm line. I watched as the excitement died from her face, and I knew my words were to blame. I hadn't realized just how fucked up I was until I saw the way she looked at me. I would give her everything I had to give, but I knew it wouldn't be enough. She wanted more. She wanted my heart and my soul, but that part of me died years ago. She'd just have to find a way to live without them. I had.

Chapter 8

How could I have been so stupid? I'd actually thought there was something between us, that he was actually falling for me, but I couldn't have been more wrong. I tried to play off his comment about not believing in love, but it stuck to me like glue and my brain just wouldn't let it go. As soon as we got back to the condo, I took the picture I'd bought and locked myself away in my room. I spent the next hour cursing myself as I laid in bed and stared at it. For a minute, I had imagined that the couple was Nathan and me. I had let myself dream, just for a moment, that one day it would be us standing on a bridge in Paris. I felt like such an idiot. I knew better than to believe in fairy tales. The longer I stared at that picture, the more I started to think that maybe he was right. Love just sets us up for disappointment. I tried to shake it off, but by the next morning I was still in a funk, and poor Max caught the brunt of my bad mood.

As usual, he was sitting at the kitchen table when I went to get my coffee. He looked up from his paper and smiled. "Good morning."

"Um hmm."

"Rough night?"

"Pfft."

"That bad, huh?"

I took my cup of coffee over to the table and sat down next to him. "Why do men have to be so damn complicated? Why can't you just be... ugh. Never mind."

He leaned back in his chair and sighed. "Ah, I get it."

"Oh, do tell," I scoffed.

"This is about Nitro."

"Nitro. Nathan. Every man on the planet. They're all a pain in the ass."

"Well, thanks for clarifying."

I rolled my eyes. "Well, it's true. I'm sure you're an ass, too. I just haven't had the luxury of witnessing it yet."

"I am." He cleared his throat as he laid down his paper and crossed his arms in irritation. "So, you don't think it's the same with women? You don't think they can be a pain in the ass, too? That they don't send mixed signals? Or lead you to think one thing, and then end up meaning something else entirely?"

"Yes, but that's different," I said sulkily.

"How?" he scoffed.

"It doesn't matter. None of it matters."

He paused for a minute. "We all have our moments, Tristen. Good and bad."

"Maybe so. I just thought things were different from what they actually are. I was hoping for something that's just not going to happen, and that's on me."

"Wow, he must have really screwed up."

"No. He didn't. He has a right to have his own feelings."

He let out a deep breath and almost growled, "Fuck."

"What? Do you know something about Nathan that you aren't telling me?"

His eyes skirted to the side. "No."

"Oh, my god. You do! You have to tell me."

"I don't *have* to tell you anything, Tristen. Besides, it's not my place to talk about it." He looked down at his watch. "Don't you have to get to work?"

"Don't try to change the subject. Please tell me."

"I can't."

"I'm stuck here, Max. I care about Nathan... I'm falling for him, and I'm beginning to wonder if that's a mistake."

"It's not a mistake." He ran his fingers through his hair with a frustrated sigh. "It's complicated. Something happened when he was younger. Something that no one should ever have to go through. He's never really gotten over it. Just try to be patient. In time, hopefully he will come around."

"What happened to him, Max?"

"Right now, that's all I can tell you. Besides, you're going to be late if you don't get a move on."

I gave him a pleading look as I stood up from the table. "Everyone has a past... and just so you know, some pretty crappy stuff has happened to me, too, Max.

But I haven't given up. I'm still here, and I'm still trying."

"So is he, but he is doing it his way… on his own terms."

"Well, his terms suck."

"I never said they didn't," he chuckled as he watched me turn and leave. Before I closed my bedroom door, I heard him shout, "Patience, Tristen. Patience."

I'd like to say that my mood got better when I got to work, but it didn't. We were busier than ever, and some guy kept hitting on me every time I went to put an order in at the bar. He was cute with his boyish charm and goofy grin. He kind of reminded me of Brad Pitt in that *Meet Joe Black* movie. Any other day, I might've been flattered that he was flirting with me, but at that moment, it was getting on my nerves. I tried to let him know that I wasn't interested, but he wasn't taking the hint. Thankfully, the lunch crowd was dying down, and it was almost time for my break. I was just about to go to the back when another group walked in. I almost kept going, but something stopped me. After a closer look, I realized why I'd hesitated. Nathan.

I couldn't take my eyes off him as Brooklyn led his group over to one of the corner booths. He was with two men, both young, maybe in their late twenties, and they were wearing casual jeans and t-shirts. There wasn't anything particularly bothersome about either of them. The two women at his side were a different story altogether. Seeing them made my stomach twist into knots, especially the particularly slutty one with her tight black tank top and scandalously short miniskirt. Just looking at her made my blood boil. As soon as Nathan sat down, she tossed her long, blonde hair over her shoulder and slid in next to him. She looked at him like she could screw him right there on the spot, and I wanted nothing more than to yank her right out of that seat. I should've just left, taken my break and let it be, but like a train wreck waiting to happen, I couldn't pull my eyes away.

After Jada took their drink order, she walked over to the bar and said something to Tony. I was waiting for his reaction when Ava came up behind me. "What's with the look? Is that guy still bugging you?"

"It's nothing. I'm just tired. I didn't get much sleep last night."

"You sure?"

"Yeah. I'm fine."

"Want something to drink? Maybe a sweet tea or…?"

"No. Really. I'm fine." I glanced back over at Nathan's table. That was a mistake. The green-eyed monster reared its ugly head as I saw the blonde bombshell whisper something in his ear. My chest tightened, and my entire body roiled with anger. I hated that feeling, but it was even worse when my insecurities started to wash over me. I couldn't help it. Every time I looked at her I saw another reason why he'd be interested in her. It wasn't just that she was attractive.

She was definitely beautiful, in a trailer-park trash kind of way, but it was more than that. She was confident and carried herself like she was the hottest thing since sliced bread. Any man would've found her appealing, which only made me second guess things between Nathan and me even more.

I was about to turn back to Ava when I noticed Nathan looking right at me. His face was completely devoid of expression. He didn't scoot away from the blonde with the undeniably fake boobs. He didn't try to push her away when she placed her hand on his arm and laughed an annoying slut-faced laugh. He did nothing but sit there and stare right back at me. "Shit."

"What?" Ava quickly turned to see who I was staring at. "Damn, girl. Don't even think about it. That's Nathan James."

"And?"

"I know he's hot and all that, but consider him *off-limits*. Trust me." She looked back at me sternly. "He's dangerous... like Bond-villain dangerous, and nobody messes with him --nobody."

"*Okay*," I said exasperatedly and held my hands up in an exaggerated surrender.

"I'm just sayin'. He's trouble. Don't go getting yourself killed over a piece of ass, girl," she laughed.

Before I had a chance to ask her how she knew he was trouble, she looked over to the bar. "Now, that guy... he's just plain adorable. You should definitely go for that."

I turned to look at him. He was still working on his gin and tonic, and that's when it hit me. I knew it was a bad idea from the minute the thought came into my head, but I just didn't care. I ignored the little warning voice as I walked over to him. Wearing my brightest smile, I placed my hand on his shoulder and asked, "Ready for another?"

His lips curled into a sexy grin. "Thanks, but I think one will do me."

"You sure? The next one's on me... as a way of saying sorry for being so distracted."

"Well, I've never been one to turn down a drink from a beautiful lady."

"Great." I called out to Tony, letting him know to bring over another round. I leaned my hip against the bar as I tucked my hair behind my ear. "Do you work around here?"

"Yeah, just around the corner at Miller and Tate."

"The lawyers' office?"

"That'd be the one. I just started there a couple of days ago."

"And they've already driven you to drinking?" I laughed.

"Not exactly." He reached for his glass and took a quick sip. "I just got my results in from the bar exam."

"So, are you here to drown your sorrows or to celebrate?"

"I don't know." He shrugged his shoulders. "I haven't opened them yet."

"You haven't opened them?"

His shaggy hair fell over his eyes as he reached into his side pocket for the envelope. "I haven't worked up the nerve to look."

"Seriously?" I'd gotten so wrapped up in our conversation that I'd almost forgotten about Nathan and his little hooker friend in the back corner. "I couldn't do it. I'd have to open it the minute I got my hands on it."

I looked over my shoulder and was surprised to see that Nathan was no longer sitting with his group. An uneasy feeling crept over me as I took a quick look around, and he was nowhere in sight. Suddenly, Joe Black's phone rang. He answered it, and after a few seconds of listening to the person on the other end, he looked at me with a strange expression on his face. "Thanks for the heads up. I'm heading that way now."

He looked away as he stood up and said, "Um, I've gotta go."

"What about your drink?"

"Maybe some other time."

Just like that, he was gone. There was still no sign of Nathan as I turned and headed towards the back. I hadn't made it far when I was suddenly pulled into a dark corner. My back pressed against the wall as Nathan stood in front of me, his fingers digging into my waist and an enraged look on his face. I was slightly dazed by the smell of his cologne and the intensity of his blue eyes, so it took me a moment to acclimate myself. Once I came to my senses, I tried to pull away from him, but his strong hands held me in place. His voice was low and full of warning as he whispered, "Tristen."

"What do you want?"

"Why don't you tell me about your friend at the bar?"

"Why don't you tell me about *yours* in the booth?"

"She's my client's girl."

"Then why the hell was she hanging all over you?"

"I can't answer that for ya. Besides, it's not my place to correct another man's woman. There was nothin' I could do about it."

"You could have moved seats. You could've brushed her off. You could've looked at her like she smelled bad... or *something*, and for your information, I was just talking to a customer, who happens to be a very nice guy."

He grumbled something under his breath, then took a step forward, pressing me further against the wall. "Let me make this perfectly clear.... I'm not interested in that chick. There's only one woman who has what I want, and it sure as hell isn't her." As he spoke, he slid his hands behind me to the small of my back. My pulse raced as I felt his hands slip down to the hem of my skirt and grab my ass with both palms. He pulled me towards him, grinding his hips into mine, and I could feel him growing hard as he said, "This hot little body of yours is *mine*." He placed his mouth close to my ear, and I gasped as the heat of his breath caressed my neck. "And nobody, and I mean *nobody* fucks with what's mine."

It was vulgar. It was crude, and I should've hated it, but I didn't. The longer he kept me pinned against the wall, the more turned on I became. I should've told him to go to hell, but I couldn't form the words. Having his hands on me, claiming me in such a demanding way, had my body reacting against my will. He'd never acted that way before, and I wasn't sure what to make of it. I did know one thing with certainty, though. If he really felt like that, he should've said something earlier instead of waiting until another guy was in play. Shaking my head, I placed my hand on his chest and gave him a shove. "Just stop. You're here with another woman for Christ's sake. I'm not yours. You don't *own me*, Nathan."

"But I do," he scoffed. He took a step back and let his eyes slowly roam over my body. "And soon... very soon... you'll be glad that I do."

With that, he turned and walked away. He gave no further explanation of who he was with or why he'd even come to the restaurant, and I stood there feeling even more frustrated. I took a deep, cleansing breath and tried to collect myself. As I stepped out of the corner, I noticed Brooklyn glaring at me. It was clear that she was pissed, but I wasn't sure if it was because she thought I was loafing or if she'd seen what had just happened with Nathan. Either way, I wasn't going to wait around to find out. I went to the bathroom to splash some cold water on my face, and when I came back out,

Nathan and his crew were gone.

My shift seemed to go on forever, and by the time I made it back to the condo, I was utterly exhausted. I laid in the bed and closed my eyes, but knowing Nathan was just a room away made it impossible to sleep. I couldn't stop thinking about the way he'd touched me. His hands were strong and forceful, and he'd looked at me like he could've devoured me right there on the spot. Even though I knew it was wrong, I found myself wanting him more than ever. Everything about him had me losing control, and I'd almost worked myself into a complete frenzy until the blonde slut flashed through my mind. Like a bucket of cold water had been thrown on my head, all those lusty thoughts vanished. I started to think about Ava's warning and the way Brooklyn had looked at me. There was more to Nathan than I'd realized, and that little voice in my head was screaming for me to get the hell out of there while I still could. But I couldn't do it. Something was holding me back, telling me that I had to listen to Max and be patient. I just prayed that he was right.

The next day, I woke up with a new resolve. I was determined to carry on with my life, do the things that I'd set out to do. Even though I knew it wouldn't be easy, I would stop being distracted by my feelings for Nathan and finish what I'd started. I didn't have to go in to work until after the lunch rush, so I had Max run me by the college. After I went by the admissions office, I took a quick tour of the campus to familiarize myself with all the different buildings. I was feeling pretty good about things as I headed into work. With a smile on my face, I walked through the front door and was immediately greeted by a not-so-happy Brooklyn. Something about her caught my attention as she stood at the counter with her hands on her hips and a scowl on her face. The scowl was nothing new, but her clothes were a different matter. As I continued walking towards her, I realized she was wearing a new uniform. The short skirt I'd become accustomed to was now replaced with a pair of long, black pants and a much less revealing, black, button-up top.

"What's with the new outfit?"

"I figured you already knew." As she looked down at the seating chart, she snarled, "The owner decided to make a change."

"Why did he do that?"

"I was going to ask you the same thing."

"Me?" Thrown by her attitude, I asked, "Why would I know?"

She crossed her arms and glared at me angrily. "Don't give me that bullshit, Tristen. We all know there's something going on with you and Nathan James."

"Nathan? What are you talking about? He doesn't have anything to do with our uniforms."

"Like you don't know." She rolled her eyes disgustedly.

"Just tell me what he has to do with the restaurant,

Brooklyn!"

"He's the *owner*."

"What?"

"Nathan James is the *owner*. Hell, he owns all of the good restaurants in town." I couldn't believe what I was hearing as she continued to drive the knife deeper into my back. "I couldn't figure out why Tony hired you in the first place. We have a waiting list a mile long with people that have actual experience, but he hired you because you're the new fling... not that *that's* going to last."

"You're wrong. He didn't even know I was coming in for the interview."

She rolled her eyes. "Of course, he did. He knows everything."

"But how?"

"Haven't you noticed all the cameras?" She motioned above us. "He knows every move we make. He's probably watching us right now."

"Shit. I'm such an idiot," I mumbled under my breath. Feeling like the rug had been yanked out from under my feet, I rushed to the bathroom and locked myself in one of the stalls. I leaned my back against the wall and stared up at the ceiling as I tried to fight the tears. I thought back to all the different warning signs— Max and his following me everywhere, Nathan's comment about love, Ava's warning about him being trouble, and the girl he brought into the restaurant. All the red flags were going up at once, and the little voice in my head was having a field day. It suddenly became hard to breathe, so I reached into my purse and grabbed my phone. I looked down at the screen, and as much as I hated to do it, there was only one person I could reach out to. Knowing she'd come through for me, I texted my sister.

Me:

I need your help.

Josie:

What's going on?

Me:

Will you come get me?

Josie:

What's wrong?

Me:

I'll explain later. Just please come get me.

Chapter 9
Nitro

As soon as I pulled up, I remembered why it had been so long since I'd been there. I fucking hated cemeteries. I hated everything about them. I looked out at all the graves, some with old, dilapidated headstones, some gleaming with new granite, and I knew the same thing lay beneath each of them—our loved ones. The people that once walked close by our side, supporting us and guiding us through time, only to leave us behind. Losing someone you love isn't the hard part. It's learning to keep living without them. It's accepting that they will never walk back through the door. It's knowing you'll never hear the sweet sound of their voice again, never feel the comfort of their embrace, and never have the security of knowing they would always catch you when you fall. It's realizing that the emptiness you feel in the pit of your stomach isn't going anywhere. It's forever a part of you. That's the hard part.

It was my father's birthday, but there was no party, no grand celebration of his fifty years of life. It was just me placing a floral spray on top of his headstone. I looked down at his name engraved in the granite, and it seemed so ordinary, nothing like my old man. He was big and boisterous, full of life, and he never met a

98

stranger. There was no way for a simple tombstone to show what kind of man he was to me. I missed his laugh, his hugs, and even the awful scent of his cheap cigars. I wished I could see him and talk to him just one more time. I wanted to tell him what he'd meant to me, but that chance would never come. When my chest became too tight to bear, I turned and started back to my car. I glanced over my shoulder, knowing Lainey was just a few feet away, but that day, I just kept walking. There'd been a time when I'd gone to see her every day. I'd talked to her and told her about whatever was on my mind, but over time, those visits happened less and less. I'd tried, but the guilt got to be too much. I was out living life, while she and my daughter were stuck in that damn hole. It should've been me lying in that grave, not her.

I got in my car and started the engine. My heart was heavy as I drove over to my mother's. I knew she was looking forward to having Colton home, but I didn't share her enthusiasm. Over the years, we'd grown distant, mainly because of my resentment towards him. Where I was determined to keep Dad's business going, he spent his time looking down on me for even trying. He'd always thought he was too good for it, even though it was the family's money that sent him to his fancy fucking college and paid for the penthouse apartment he'd been living in for the past ten years.

When I pulled up to Mom's apartment, Colton's Mercedes was right up front. It wasn't the best way to start things off, but I swallowed my annoyance and headed inside. As usual, Mom was bustling around the kitchen getting things ready. She looked up at me and smiled.

"There you are!" She shuffled over and gave me a big hug. While my mother had survived the attack, she hadn't come out of it completely unscathed. The bullet had nicked her spine and caused slight paralysis in her left leg. It was one of the reasons she'd decided to sell the house. The thought of adding ramps and widening the doors just hadn't appealed to her. As soon as she was able, we'd put the house on the market and started looking for a new place for her to live. She'd decided on one of the upscale assisted living communities on the edge of town. It was quiet, and the apartment she'd liked was on the ground floor. It was just right for her, and she was happy. That was all that mattered to me.

She was still hugging me when she asked, "You okay?"

"Yeah, I'm good. Got Dad taken care of."

"That's good. Thank you, sweetheart." She looked up at me with tears in her eyes. "I know it would mean a lot to him."

Feeling the need to change the subject, I stepped back and smiled. "It smells great in here."

"I hope you're hungry. I made fried chicken."

"With mashed potatoes?"

"Of course. I know how you love them. It's almost ready. Why don't you go say hello to your brother? He and Angela are in the living room."

"Angela?" It seemed like every time Colton came over, he brought a different chick with him. "Is she a new girl?"

She shook her head and said, "No, Nate. She's the same young lady he brought home a few months ago. He seems to really like her."

I leaned forward and peered through the doorway, trying to get a look at her. "Yeah, I remember her." She was cute with her red hair and emerald green eyes, but she wasn't the kind of girl he usually dated. She actually seemed to have a little character about her. "She's a teacher or something, right?"

"No, that was Tina. Angela is a nurse practitioner."

"Stepping up his game, huh?" I teased as I reached for a chicken leg and took a bite. "Damn. These are even better than last time."

"You're going to ruin your lunch." She batted me away as she said, "Now, go say hi to your brother."

"Yes, boss." With the chicken leg still in my hand, I started for the living room. Colton was sprawled out on the sofa watching the news, while Angela was staring down at her phone.

Colton glanced up at me and gave me one of his phony smiles. "Hey there, little bro. Good to see ya."

"You, too," I said as I sat down in the recliner.

"Mom said you went by the cemetery this morning."

"I did."

"It had to be tough to go today of all days."

"Yeah. Wasn't easy," I grumbled. "You ever think about going out there?"

"Nah, man. You know how I feel about all that. I hate to think of him like that."

"And I don't?" I muttered under my breath. I was starting to get frustrated, so I turned to Angela. "Good to see you again, Angela."

Her green eyes seemed to sparkle as she looked up to me and smiled. "It's really good to see you again, Nathan. I'm so sorry about your loss. Did the police ever catch the men who did it?"

"No." The cops weren't any help in finding the DeMarco brothers, but I'd never expected them to be. Knowing there would be blowback for killing my father, they had skipped town. Leaving was the only smart thing they'd done. Murray and I had continued to hunt for them. We'd started with Drake Martin, since he had been helping them expand their business. When he hadn't given us the information we needed, we ended him, sending a message to all the assholes tied to the DeMarco brothers. We went through every single connection they had and dealt with them accordingly, but none of them had panned out. Over the years, there had been several DeMarco sightings, but they'd always managed to slip through the cracks. Eventually the trail had gone cold, but I had never given up searching. In time, I knew they'd slip up, and when they did, I'd be there waiting.

"I hate to hear that. I'm sure he meant a lot to you."

"He did."

Colton sat up on the sofa as he reached for the remote and lowered the volume on the TV. "Did you see the game last week?"

There was a time when my brother and I were fairly close. We could actually talk without thinking about what we were saying, but since my father's death, every word was forced, and it was difficult for us to have a simple conversation. "I missed it."

"It was a hell of game. Kershaw was on fire."

I couldn't remember the last time I'd watched the Dodgers play. I didn't have the time... or the interest. Even though I couldn't have cared less, I told him, "Hate I missed it."

"We should try to meet up for a game sometime."

Knowing that would never happen, I nodded. "Yeah, we could do that."

"I'll look into getting us some tickets." He looked over to Angela and gave her a wink. "Maybe we could go before the wedding."

"Wedding?"

"Angela and I are going to get married next month."

"Well, how about that? Colton James is getting married. Never thought I'd see the day."

"What about you? You have anyone special these days?"

Tristen's face came flashing into my thoughts. She

gave me peace just by thinking about her smile, the scent of her hair, and the softness of her touch, and I almost considered telling him about her. Then, I realized he'd have questions, and my mother would, too. I wasn't ready to answer them. I wasn't sure I would ever be ready, so I decided against it. "No one worth mentioning."

"You should do something about that. You aren't getting any younger," he chuckled.

Before I had a chance to respond to his douchebag comment, Mom called out from the kitchen. "It's ready when you are."

Wasting no time, I stood up and headed into the kitchen. She'd made one hell of a spread: fried chicken, mashed potatoes, homemade biscuits, greens, and a pie waiting on the stove. Colton came up behind me and leaned over the table. "Damn, Mom. You outdid yourself."

"Well, we're celebrating. I'm so excited for you both." She gave him a hug and then reached for Angela, giving her a hug as well. "I wish your father was here to see this."

"Me, too. I think he'd like her."

"Oh, I know he would."

He reached for Angela's hand, leading her over to the table. Once she was seated, he sat down beside her. "I haven't told you about the house we're thinking of buying. I think you'll like it. It has four big bedrooms, and it's right on the lake. We'll even have our own dock. I can't wait for you to see it."

"I'm sure it's beautiful, Colton."

"Hmmm... A house by the lake... Sounds expensive." Colton didn't miss that my tone was filled with sarcasm. He gave me a scathing look as he reached for the bowl of potatoes.

"We've been putting money back for months."

"So, you won't be needing any helping buying it then?" I pushed. I knew I was being an asshole, but I didn't fucking care. There was no way he could cover it all, not with his job. In time, his degree in accounting would pay off, but he hadn't been working long enough yet to make a name for himself.

"Not exactly."

Mom gave me a warning look as she handed me the plate of chicken. "You know we'll be glad to help any way we can. You just let us know what you need us to do, sweetheart."

"Thanks, Mom." I could almost see the dollar signs flashing through his mind as he filled his plate with food. "We'd appreciate that."

Angela placed her hand on Colton's as she looked over at me. "It really is something.... It needs a little work, but we're hoping to have everything done before the baby comes."

The room quickly fell silent as Colton and Mom waited for my reaction. If I'd found out the news a few weeks ago, I might've felt differently. I wasn't exactly thrilled, but I didn't wish him ill. Everyone deserved their chance at a family. I'd had mine, but I blew it. Hopefully, he wouldn't make the same mistake. "You've got a kid on the way?"

"We do. It's still early yet." He placed his hand on her belly. "She isn't due for another six months or so."

"Well, congratulations to you both."

"Thanks, Nathan. I appreciate that." He looked over to Mom. "Maybe you could come stay with us for a little while when the baby comes."

Mom smiled as she answered, "I would love that."

Once the door was open, Colton couldn't stop talking about their plans for the wedding, the baby, and the house. He really was settling down, and he seemed happy about it. Just as we were finishing up the last of the pie, he turned his attention back to me. "What about you? Are you doing okay?"

"Couldn't be better." I slid my chair back from the table and stood. Before he had a chance to push for more, I took my dishes over to the sink. "Mom, lunch was great, but I've gotta get back to work."

"Are you sure you can't stay a little longer?" she pleaded.

"I wish I could, but Murray's waiting on me back at the office." I gave her a quick kiss on the forehead, then turned to Colton and Angela. "Congratulations to you both. I'm really happy for you."

"Thanks, Nathan," Angela smiled.

Colton stood up and walked over to me, wrapping his arms tightly around me as he gave me a hug. "Keep in touch, okay? And think about coming to one of those games with me."

"We'll see."

I said my final goodbyes, then I headed out to my truck. I closed the door and sat there for a moment, enjoying the complete and utter silence. I needed a moment to calm the storm that was raging inside my head. I tried to shake it, but the longer I sat there, the louder the thoughts became. I was already on edge, trying to fight the feelings brewing inside of me, when my cell started to ring. Knowing how Mom felt about cell phones, I'd left it in the car, so I had no idea that Tony had been trying to reach me.

"What's up?"

"It's Tristen."

"What about her?"

He cleared his throat before he answered. "I'm sure everything's fine and all, but…."

"Spit it out, Tony."

"She left."

"Okay. And?"

"She was alone."

"Come again?" I growled. The day just kept getting better and better.

"I didn't even know she was leaving, Nitro. One of the girls came up to me after she'd already gone. She said Tristen had something to take care of."

"And she didn't call Max."

"No. She went out the back."

"Fuck!" My grip tightened on the phone as I asked, "Did something happen?"

"Hell, I don't know. You know how these women can be. There's no telling what rattled her."

"Any idea where she was headed?"

"One of the girls said they saw her heading over towards the coffee shop, but she's not there now. You want me to call Max?"

"No. *I'll* take care of it."

Chapter 10
Tristen

Before I left the restaurant, I told Ava that something had come up and I had to leave. She was hesitant, but she agreed to wait a few minutes before she let Tony or the others know I'd gone. I wasn't sure if Brooklyn was being completely honest about the surveillance cameras, but either way, I wasn't taking any chances. Trying my best not to be seen, I slipped out the back door and headed over to the alley behind the coffee shop. I'd been waiting about forty-five minutes when Josie pulled up.

As soon as I got in her car, Josie gave me a worried look, and I almost regretted calling her as I heard the concern in her voice. "Are you okay?"

"Yes, Josie. I'm fine." I gave her a quick smile. "I'm just not feeling well."

"Are you sick?"

"No. It's nothing like that. It's just a headache. I haven't been sleeping very well."

"Tristen…"

"Please, don't start," I cut her off. "It's just a headache. Don't read anything more into it."

"Okay." She turned her attention to the road as she pulled out of the parking lot. "Do you want me to take you over to Nitro's place?"

"Um… no."

"Then, where do you want to go?"

"Can you just drive around for a minute?"

"Sure, but I have class in a little while."

We hadn't been driving long when I finally worked up the courage to ask her, "Do you still have your apartment?"

I knew she had moved in with Big Mike a few weeks ago. She'd met him when she came to the Satan's Fury clubhouse looking for me. They'd worked closely with Nathan to bring me back home. When she finally admitted that she'd fallen for Big, I wasn't surprised. He was one of the good ones, a man who'd move heaven and earth for the people he cared about, and there was no doubt he cared about my sister. You could see it in his eyes whenever he looked at her, and she felt the same way about him. It made sense for them to move in together. I just hoped she still had her place in town.

"Yes, but I've moved most of my things over to Big's place."

"Do you still have a bed and stuff there?"

"What's going on, Tristen?" Over the years, I'd given my sister plenty of reasons to worry about me. When our parents had died, I'd made some bad choices, hurting the people that cared most about me. I was broken-hearted, and I took it out on those closest to me, especially her. But in time, I managed to move on from my past and made a life for myself. I had just been coming into my own when I was kidnapped. Once I was rescued, she was there with me at the counseling center. We finally had a chance to talk, really talk, and we mended our broken relationship. I didn't want to jeopardize that, but I just didn't have it in me to tell her about everything—at least not yet.

"I'm fine. Really. I am. I just need some time to clear my head." I tried to reassure her, but she wasn't buying it. "With everything that's been going on with work and trying to get enrolled in my classes, I haven't had time to think."

"You're sure that's it? You've been through so much. You know you can talk to me."

"There's nothing to talk about, Josie. I'm just tired and need some time to myself."

"Okay, but I'm here if you need anything."

"I know."

When we got to her apartment, she took me upstairs and showed me where everything was. As she handed me the keys, she asked, "Do you want me to go grab you some groceries? Maybe some milk and cereal?"

"No. I'm good."

"Okay. I'll come by and check on you tomorrow."

"Thanks for all this."

"No problem."

She turned and started for the door. Before she stepped outside, I asked, "Can you do me one more favor?"

"Sure."

"Can you keep this between us? Don't tell Big I'm

here."

Doubt washed over her face as she asked, "Why?"

"Well, the whole point of being here is so I can clear my head. I can't really do that if everyone knows I'm here."

"I don't know, Tristen."

"Please. Just for a couple of days."

"Okay, but I don't like it."

When she finally left, I went to her old bedroom and curled up on the bed. I couldn't believe how quickly things had spun out of control. Just a few days ago, I'd thought things were going well, that Nathan and I were figuring things out, but slowly, the thread that had been holding us together had started to unravel. I was angry with him. I might've felt differently if he'd just been honest with me, but he chose to treat me like a possession instead of an actual human being. I'd known better, but I'd ignored my instincts. It was time for me to stop feeling sorry for myself. I had to remember that the past was just that-- the past. Even after all I'd been through, I was still standing, still fighting, and I wasn't going to let Nathan James get the best of me.

I had to accept the fact that things with Nathan were not going to be the way I'd thought they'd be. He was handsome, strong, and powerful, but Nathan was no knight in shining armor. He was damaged and broken beyond repair. He had control issues, and he was an all-around pain in the ass. Yes, he had his issues, but despite my better judgement, I was falling for him. I knew it was a bad idea. I knew there was something different about Nathan. Even before Max had told me, I'd known something awful had happened to him. I could see it in his eyes, but there was more to him than the man created from pain and heartbreak. There were times, like the night we stayed up talking in my room or our lunch at the Shack, where I'd gotten a glimpse of the man he didn't share with the rest of the world. His walls were down, and he wasn't pushing me away. I wanted more of that man, the man who had captured my heart, but then again, I'd always tended to gravitate to those things that were just beyond my reach. I had to remind myself that there was another side to him. I had to find a way to handle both sides, without losing myself in the process.

For starters, I needed to get back to work. Maybe Nathan had been the reason I'd gotten my job, but I was good at it. I made good money there, and I liked the people I worked with, even Brooklyn. I wasn't going to walk away from it just because Nathan had gotten me the job. I was going to stick with it, save my money, and get enrolled in classes. And at some point in the near future, I needed to find a place of my own.

Feeling more determined than ever, I got up out of bed, grabbed my phone, and called a cab. Thinking it was best to meet the cab at the front of the building, I quickly gathered my things. With my mind focused on getting to work, I opened the door, but I was stopped dead in my tracks as I found Nathan standing at the top of the stairs. When he turned to look at me, I groaned.

"Seriously? You really need to get a hobby."

He had no response. He just stood there silently staring at me. His expression was blank, but his eyes…. His eyes were filled with angst. It was clear that he had something to say, but he held on to his words and left me to wonder what he was thinking. When I'd had enough of his silent treatment, I started to walk past him. "I've got to get to work."

As I walked by him, he reached for my arm, gently stopping me before I started down the steps. His voice was dripping with warning as he growled, "Tristen."

"What?"

He stood over me, just inches away, and my heart began to thump a little harder. Damn. Why did he have to be so freaking hot? I was furious with him, and yet, I still felt an undeniable pull towards him. I wanted to touch him, to feel his arms around me and his mouth on my skin, and I had no doubt that he knew how I felt. It was written all over my face every time I laid eyes on him. Trying to ignore my traitorous hormones, I crossed my arms and looked him directly in the eye.

"You might think this is some kind of game we're playing here, that I'm just some pawn you can play with, but you're wrong, Nathan. This is no game, because I refuse to play."

"You're not just some pawn, Tristen. You're the fucking queen, the most powerful piece in the game." He took a step towards me, placing his hands on my waist as he closed the gap between us. "Maybe you didn't know, but it's your job to protect the king."

"Oh, please," I scoffed. "Who am I protecting *you* from?"

His eyes pierced straight through me, pulling at my heart as he stared at me. "Myself."

His answer hung in the air, looming over me as I tried to comprehend what he'd just said. I lowered my eyes to the ground as I replied, "I don't know, Nathan. The odds are stacked against me. I'm not sure I can win."

"It's not always about winning, Angel. Sometimes you have to take a step back and look at things from a different angle before you make your next move."

"Why am I the queen? What makes me so different?"

He looked over his shoulder as he took in a deep breath. "There was a time when I felt everything... the good and the bad, but then it got to be too much, so I stopped feeling altogether. I became numb, and I learned to just get through the day... to just exist."

"I'm not sure I understand."

"I don't understand it myself, but you triggered something in me the night we came for you. I didn't ask for it... I didn't want it, but there it was." He brought his hands up to my face, and his thumb lightly caressed my cheek as he spoke. "You were a force I couldn't ignore. I couldn't walk away from you, even if it meant risking everything."

"I know something happened to you. I don't know what it was or who it involved." I placed my hands on his chest as I leaned towards him. "Will you tell me?"

"Someday."

It wasn't the answer I was hoping for, but he didn't said no. "Okay."

There comes a time in a girl's life when she has to decide if she's going to fight for what she wants or just walk away. That was my moment, and it wasn't an easy decision. I knew moving forward with Nathan wasn't going to be easy. He was broken, damaged by a past that I knew nothing about, and his issues weren't easily ignored. The little voice in my head whispered, *Give him a chance*, and that was exactly what I was going to do.

I reached for his hand and pulled him inside Josie's apartment, locking the door behind us. Without speaking, I led him past the kitchen, through the living room, and into the bedroom. I remained silent as I wound my arms around his neck, pulling him closer as I pressed my lips against his. I wasn't sure if the timing was right, or if I was ready to take the next step with him, but I did know I wanted it to be on my terms, not something dictated by him. Just that once, I wanted to be the one in control.

I took a step towards him, but he didn't move. He knew what was coming, what I wanted from him. He'd told me I was his, that he wanted me in his bed, and I was about to take him at his word. "For just a little

while, forget about the past, and just be here with me…
Feel this with me."

I never took my eyes off his as I slowly started to unbutton his black collared shirt. I'd envisioned that moment so many times, yet when the time came, I was overcome with nerves and desire all at once. I eased the shirt over his shoulders and let it drop to the floor. My fingers trailed down his chest, roaming ever so slowly over the defined muscles of his abdomen. His heart beat rapidly against his chest, and I knew he was working hard to restrain himself. He knew what I needed, and he was giving it to me. My hands dropped to my waist as I reached for the hem of my t-shirt. I pulled it over my head, and his eyes shimmered with need as he stood there gazing at me.

Just looking at him made it hard to breathe, hard to think, and the way his eyes filled with lust when he looked at me only increased my need for him. I lowered my mouth to his neck, lightly kissing him as I whispered, "Nathan."

His hand slipped into my hair, gently pulling as his mouth hovered over mine. Just before our lips touched, he paused. His gorgeous blue eyes fell on me, searching for some kind of confirmation, but I was too impatient to wait. I pushed up onto my tiptoes, crashing my mouth against his. My body melted into him as he wrapped his arms around my waist and pressed me close to his chest. I couldn't remember ever wanting anything so much.

The tips of his fingers trailed along my spine, and I

arched towards him, seeking the heat of his touch. As we continued to kiss, my body became heated, smoldering as warmth spread through me. It had started with just a spark, but it had continued to build, intensifying with every touch. He slid his hands behind me and effortlessly released the clasp of my bra before bringing the tips of his fingers to the straps and gently brushing them off my shoulders. I shivered with anticipation as I felt the palm of his hand linger over my bare flesh. The lace fabric slipped ever so slowly down my body, eventually puddling uselessly around my feet. He looked down at me, sending chills through my body as his eyes roamed over every inch of my exposed skin.

"You have no fucking idea what you do to me," he whispered as he ran his rough, calloused fingers across my back.

A rush of heat rolled against my skin as he stood there staring at me, appraising me. There was no doubt that he wanted me. I saw it in his eyes, felt it in his touch, and I felt the same about him. He was my every desire, all my secret fantasies wrapped into one, and he was about to be mine. I laid my hand on his chest, feeling his heart beat fast and hard. I was relieved that I wasn't the only one who felt the overwhelming need. Like me, he'd felt every spark, every flicker of heat that surged through our bodies.

"Tell me," I pleaded.

"You make me want to be better."

I kissed him again, but not gently like before.

Instead, it was hot, passionate, and demanding. Desire surged through me as I unfastened his belt buckle. With only one thought on my mind, I lowered his pants over his hips and down his legs to remove them and tossed them onto the bed. I felt brazen and powerful as I placed my hands on his chest and gave him a light shove, forcing him down on the mattress. My body practically hummed as I looked down at him. Damn. He was something to behold. I couldn't have dreamed up a sexier image as he lay there looking at me like I was a meal he was about to devour. Knowing I was enjoying the scenery, his lips curled into a smirk. That smile took the last of my restraint, and my impatience took over. His eyes widened with anticipation as I gradually lowered my zipper, taking my time to ease my jeans and panties down my hips. I tossed them to the side as I started towards the bed, but stopped when he demanded, "Wait."

Chapter 11
Nitro

I'd spent years building a tower of thick, protective walls around me, guarding myself from pain and heartbreak, but the foundation was starting to crumble, bit by bit. No matter how hard I tried to fight it, to secure them in place, I could feel them crashing down around me. I looked up at her, staring at me with love in her eyes, and I found myself feeling things I'd forbidden myself to feel. I knew the risk, knew I was standing close to the edge, and I had to fight the urge to walk out that door. I didn't ask for her to love me, to heal me, but there she was putting the pieces back together. She made it seem easy, like she was meant to be mine, and I was beginning to believe there was more to our connection than I'd ever realized. There was no doubt that I wanted her, but having her came at a cost. The walls would have to come down, but then again, maybe I'd been waiting for her to break them down all along. She was getting to me in a way that I hadn't expected. When I looked at her and saw those beautiful blue eyes staring back at me, I knew living without her wasn't a life I wanted to live, and it scared the hell out of me.

With a metaphorical chisel in her hand, she stood at the edge of the bed with lust-filled eyes. I'd thought she was done working on my walls, but she was just getting started. "Nathan."

My eyes slowly roamed over her perfect round breasts, the seductive curve of her hips, and her long, lean legs. Fuck. She had every nerve in my body itching to feel her. I wanted her, all of her, but I needed to know that she was ready. "Are you sure about this?"

Her eyes locked on mine as she took a step forward and lowered herself down on the mattress, straddling me. "Absolutely. Are you?"

My hands suddenly became rough and impatient as they ran up her back, pulling her towards me. The feel of her mouth against mine made the blood rush to my cock, immediately fueling my need to have her-- all of her. Her fingers tangled in my hair, pulling me towards her as I lowered my mouth to her breast. Heavy breaths and low moans filled the room as I flicked my tongue against her nipple. Her head fell back, and there was no doubt that she liked having my mouth on her. I wanted to go farther, to explore every inch of her body, to taste her and watch her come apart, but it wasn't my time. She wanted to be in control, and I was trying my best to let her have it. But giving up complete control had never come easily for me.

Goosebumps prickled across her skin as my hand slid between her legs. I trailed my fingers across the vulnerable line between her thigh and center while my other hand cupped her breast, my thumb stroking her nipple as I added more fuel to the fire burning between us. She rocked her hips forward as she dragged her center across my throbbing cock, and I thought I'd lose my mind if I had to wait another minute to be inside her. An overwhelming need to extinguish the burn had me struggling to contain my craving for her. I'd never wanted anyone as much as I wanted her in that moment. My lips left her mouth and slowly traveled down her long, slender neck. Releasing her for only a second, I reached beside me for my slacks. I pulled a condom from my wallet, and as soon as I slid it on, she was back on me, centering herself on top of me. She hovered over me, and the heat of our breaths mingled between us until the anticipation became too much.

"I've imagined having you like this, Tristen. Night after night." My hand snaked up her spine. "You've thought about it, too. Haven't you? You've thought about what it'd feel like to have me deep inside you, making you come... fucking you senseless."

With a sharp intake of breath, she answered, "I think about it all the time."

My hand dove into her hair, grasping at the nape of her neck as I delved deeper into her mouth, our tongues twisting and tasting each other with all the passion and desire we'd kept bottled up for weeks. Her mouth was warm and soft, and each twirl of her tongue made my cock grow even harder. My breath became strained as I tried to fight the temptation to take control. Sensing my struggle, she released my mouth and rocked her hips forward. She arched her back as I placed my hands on her hips to guide her over my cock. Her hand lowered between us as she took me in her hand, slowly stroking me. A fevered hiss slipped through her lips as she slowly inched down over me, taking me deep.

Bliss. Pure bliss. I'd had no idea it would feel so good, and I wanted to savor every second. I wanted to let myself feel every erotic sensation, but the building need became too much. A deep growl vibrated through my chest as her pace quickened, but I needed more. Unable to control myself, I brought my hands up to her hips, guiding her back and forth. Her nails dug into my chest as her hips bucked against mine, meeting every thrust with more force, more intensity. I could feel the pressure building as her walls constricted around me. Sensing that I needed more, the shift of her hips became more demanding with every move. I'd wanted to take things slow, but my cock had other plans. Teetering close to the edge, I dug my fingertips into her hips and held on, bracing myself for the next wave that crashed through my body. With one last deep thrust, her body became tense, and her breath stilled as her head fell back. Her orgasm took hold as she clamped down around me, making it impossible to hold back as she continued to buck against me. The fire that had raged inside me consumed me as I came deep inside her. "Fuck."

I held on to her hips, holding her in place as I caught my breath. Her body trembled above me, still shuddering from the explosion of pleasure. Seconds later, her body collapsed on top of mine, her head on my chest and her heart next to mine. The rapid beating of her heart began to slow and eventually returned to normal, but she didn't move. I ran my fingers through her hair as I whispered, "Better than I could've imagined."

She raised her head and smiled as she said, "I didn't know it would be like this."

"Is that a good thing?"

"Oh, yeah. It's definitely a good thing." Her lips pressed against mine, and I immediately felt the heat of desire returning in my abdomen. The woman was going to be the death of me. Before I had a chance to protest, she slowly lifted herself off me and rushed into the bathroom. While she was gone, I disposed of the condom and grabbed us both a glass of water. When I walked back into the room, she was hurrying around, gathering her clothes in her arms.

"Whoa. What are you doing?"

"I told you... I have to get to work," she answered without looking at me. She slipped on her panties and then moved on to her bra.

"What's the rush? I think Tony can manage without you for a few more hours." Smiling, I walked over to her and placed my hands on her hips. "Besides, I'm not done with you."

"Sorry, but no can do." She blew me off as she quickly pressed her lips against mine, then pulled her shirt over her head and smiled. "I don't want the owner to have any regrets about hiring me."

"Is that right?"

"Yep. The word on the street is he can be a real hard ass about taking off without good reason, and being late is like a death sentence."

"Nothing wrong with having high expectations."

"True, but apparently this guy takes it to a whole new level." Her teeth toyed with her bottom lip as she tried to keep herself from smiling. "From what the girls have said, he's super good looking, but we're all starting to think he's gay."

"*Gay*?" I had to clear my throat to stop myself from choking. "What makes you say that?"

"You've seen the bar. It has this clean, modern feel. Kind of fancy. Not your typical macho man kind of place, and then there was this thing with our uniforms…" She scratched the edge of her ear as her eyes skirted towards the floor. "Out of the blue, he changed our cute, little outfits to these god-awful things with pants. They look ridiculous. I can see why everyone thinks he's gay."

There was no doubt that she was goading me. I wasn't sure when or how she'd found out that I owned the West End bar. I mean, it wasn't exactly a secret, but I hadn't actually come out and told her. I hadn't wanted her to think I was the reason she got the job. The truth was, I wasn't. She'd managed to get it all on her own. If I'd had my way, she would have been working somewhere else, away from any business of mine, but it was clear that she was pleased with herself for getting the job. Since it meant something to her, I'd left it alone. "So, what you're saying is… you don't like these new uniforms?"

"No. They're awful, and it's not just me. The other girls hate them, too. Wearing those things is going to kill our tips."

I leaned forward and kissed her on the lips before I turned and started picking up my clothes. As I began getting dressed, I told her, "I'll take care of it."

"Thanks, boss. I'd appreciate that." She straightened the covers on the bed, trying to get it back the way it'd been when we got there, then waited as I finished getting dressed. "You ready?"

I nodded and followed her towards the door. Just before she opened it, I reached for her, pulling her close to me as I said, "Just so we're clear, when you get off tonight, you come to my room… I want you in my bed so I can finish what you started here."

"It will be late."

"I'll be waiting."

A sexy smirk curled across her face as she said, "If you say so."

"Now, she's learning," I teased.

She playfully rolled her eyes as she started for the door. "You're too much."

"You have no idea." I opened the door for her and smiled. "But you're about to find out."

I dropped her off at work and headed into the office. It was getting late, and I needed to check in with

Murray. We'd been contacted by a potential new buyer, a heavy hitter, and Murray was set on us taking him on. I was leery, but I knew a guy like him would more than make up for our losses with Satan's Fury. When I got to the warehouse, it was quiet, but Murray's truck was still parked up front. As soon as I walked in the office, Murray looked up to me and growled, "Where the hell have you been?"

"I told you I had things to do."

"All fucking day?" He tugged at his gray beard and huffed. "You know Dayton has been waiting on your call."

"I'll get to Dayton."

"When exactly do you plan to get to him? Today? Tomorrow? Next fucking week?" The wrinkles in his face were more pronounced, making him look even older as he frowned at me.

"I'm not jumping into bed with this guy until I know who the hell we're dealing with. We don't know shit about him."

"That's bullshit, and you know it. We know everything there is to know about him. Ryder gave you the file on him days ago. What else do you need to know?"

"Come on, Murray. You know how this works." I walked over to my desk and sat down. "It's not just him we're dealing with. It's all the motherfuckers he's working with and who he's selling to. We've gotta play this thing smart, or we don't play at all."

He paused a minute and sighed. "You're right. I was getting ahead of myself."

"Yeah, you were," I taunted. "We'll get it sorted. I'll schedule a meet with him for mid-week. That'll give us time to look into things a bit more before we make any final decisions about this guy."

"Want me to go with you?"

"I'll take Ryder or Max. You stay here and keep an eye on things."

"You got it." He paused again, and then asked, "What about this morning? Did everything go okay?"

My father and Murray had grown up together. They were just a couple of teenagers when they'd decided to go into business together. Neither of them had had any idea what they were getting into, but together they'd figured it out. They weren't just partners; they were best friends. It had been hard on Murray when we lost my dad, harder than any of us had ever realized. I looked up at him to see the worry on his face and answered, "It went good. I went by to see him at the gravesite, and then stopped by Mom's. Colton was there."

"And how is he these days?"

Murray didn't hold the same grudge against Colton that I had. He seemed to understand why he'd decided against working with us. "Turns out he's getting married. He's got a kid on the way."

"Well, good for him. Good to see that things are working out for him. Maybe someday you'll follow suit."

"*Murray,*" I warned.

"I know. I know. But at some point, you're gonna have to find a way to let go of what's gone, and be grateful for what still remains." He stood up and grabbed his keys. "Well, I better get to the house. Kathryn will have my ass if I'm late to dinner."

As soon as he was gone, I put a call in to Dayton and set up a meet with him for later in the week. Like Murray, he was eager to get things rolling. His dealer had been shut down, leaving him in the lurch with buyers on his back. Time wasn't on his side, and he needed to move forward as soon as possible. I, on the other hand, was in no rush. I had a bad feeling about the guy, especially since his dealer had just been busted, and I was in no hurry to get involved with him. I had my doubts that the cops were done investigating, and in time, I was sure they'd connect the dots right back to Dayton. Dealing with the cops was nothing new. It came with the territory, but it was a matter of playing it safe, not adding any unnecessary heat to an already fiery situation.

I'd just finished booking my flight when Ryder barged into the office. With his fierce expression, he looked like he was about to blow. As he stepped closer, I could feel the tension radiating off him. "We've got a problem."

I learned a long time ago, you're only as good as the men you have working by your side. Ryder was big, brawny, and tough as nails. His bite wasn't something

I'd trained him in. He'd been like that since the first day I'd met him. I'd taken him on when he was fresh out of high school. He'd grown up hard, rebellious, and full of anger, but as I'd quickly learned, he was dependable, and I could trust him. In our line of work, with the kind of goods and money we had trading hands, trust was a hard thing to come by. In all the years he'd been working with me, he'd never let me down. So, when he came to me with a problem, I knew it was important.

"What kind of problem?"

"There's one hell of a storm out in the Bering. Looks like we're going to lose the load."

"Fuck." Losing a load was a double hit for us. Not only would we lose the artillery, we'd lose the timber. "Is this the Wentworth load?"

"The one and only." He turned his head as he cleared his throat. "The storm's pretty fucking rough, man. They're calling in the Coast Guard."

"They need to dump it. *Now*. The last thing we need is the Coast Guard to start nosing around that fucking timber."

"I'll take care of it."

He made the call and assured me that he'd make sure things were handled. I'd thought I was done putting out fires for the day, but as it turned out, I was just getting started.

Chapter 12

By the time I made it back to work, the dinner rush was in full effect. The place was a madhouse; all the tables were full, and the bar was packed, making me feel even more guilty for leaving like I had. I should've been there, and I hated that I'd left them in the lurch. I rushed into the staff room, put on the ridiculous new uniform, and started towards the front. When I walked by the bar, it was clear to see that Tony was struggling. Several customers were leaning over the bar, complaining, and calling out his name. He was trying his best, but it was a lot, even for the most experienced bartender. Without asking, I slipped through the counter gate and got to work. I took orders and served the drinks I knew how to make, leaving the others up to Tony. The pace was hectic with no time for mistakes. I was a little frazzled, but I loved it. In a matter of minutes, Tony was caught back up, and it was time for me to go back out front. I started through the gate, but I stopped when Tony called out to me.

"Yeah?"

"Thanks for the hand."

I smiled. "Anytime."

"I'm glad to see that you're back, but don't pull that shit again. If you need to leave, you come to me."

"Understood. I'm really sorry about that."

"Come in early tomorrow. It's time to start training you to run the bar."

I'd been wanting to get behind the bar since the first day I'd started, and there was no hiding my eagerness. "Really? That would be awesome."

"Don't get too excited," he chuckled. "It's going to take a lot of work, and maybe even some classes if you choose to stick with it. Now, get your ass to work before Brooklyn has a come-apart."

"On it."

After I sorted my tables with Brooklyn, I went straight to work. Even with the large crowd and constant back and forth to the kitchen, I couldn't get my mind off Nathan. I hadn't expected things to take such a dramatic turn, especially after how I'd felt earlier in the day. But I'd taken a step back, looked at things from a different angle, and I'd found a glimmer of hope that things might just work out. I was happy, and apparently smiling like the Cheshire Cat when Ava came up behind me.

"So, I'm guessing things are better now," she teased. "You look downright delighted, which is surprising after the way you jetted out of here."

"Yes, things are better."

"Are you going to tell me what happened, or am I going to have to guess?" When I didn't answer, she gave me a mischievous look. "Well, if you ask me, it looks like my girl got laid, but then again… it could've been one hell of a margarita, the kind that makes you forget all your troubles. If it's just a margarita, I'm gonna need to know where I can get me some of that."

"Let's just say I was upset about a few things, and now, those things don't seem to be as important as they were a few hours ago."

"Yep, you got laid. So, who's the guy? I didn't realize you were seeing someone."

"Aren't you full of questions today?"

"Come on, you've gotta give me a little something. Between work and school, I haven't been on a date in months. Hell, I haven't even watched a good chick flick in weeks. My sex life has withered away to nothing. Let me live vicariously."

A part of me wanted to tell her everything, from beginning to end. I hadn't talked to anyone about Nathan, not even Josie, and it wasn't easy keeping it all bottled up inside. I wanted to tell her how my heart skipped a beat whenever he looked at me, how I could feel him even when he wasn't in the room, and how just the sound of his voice soothed my ravaged soul. I wanted to tell her everything, but I couldn't get her warning out of my head. She'd told me that Nathan was off limits, and while I had no idea why she'd said it, I doubted she'd understand. "It's complicated."

"I'm good with complicated. That just means there's more meat to the story. Dish it."

"Have you ever met someone that makes you feel like you're the most important thing in their world?

Like you have something special inside of you that you never knew existed?"

"Um... No."

"Well, it's an unbelievable feeling. Don't settle for anything less, Ava."

With that, I turned and got back to work. The rush never slowed, making the night seem to fly by. Before I knew it, I was in the car with Max on the way back to the condo. He was quiet, even more quiet than usual, which made me wonder if something was wrong. I was tempted to ask, but before I had the chance, he'd pulled up in the parking garage and gotten out of the car. He walked over to me, opening my door, and then led me over to the elevator. The question lingered on my tongue, just waiting for me to ask, but something told me to leave it. When we got to the top floor and the elevator doors opened, I turned to him and said, "Thanks, Max."

He nodded, and then he was gone. When I walked inside the condo, the lights were on, but there was no sign of Nathan. I hadn't forgotten that he expected me to come to his room. In fact, it'd been on my mind every moment since I'd left him earlier, but I was in need of a hot shower. I went straight to my bathroom, turned on the water, and as soon as I was undressed, I stepped inside. I hadn't even washed my hair when I heard the shower door squeak open. My breath caught in my throat as I saw a naked Nathan standing there in all his wondrous glory. The water trickled down his chest as he stepped towards me. His eyes were filled with desire as he growled, "I've been waiting for you."

I loved that look in his eye. He looked at me like I was the sun, and everything revolved around me. I thought back to him telling me that he didn't buy into love, but there was something in his eyes that gave me doubt. "I hoped you would be."

His hands slipped around my waist as he leaned towards me and pressed his lips firmly against mine. The kiss was hungry and full of desire as he pulled me closer. I wound my arms around his neck as his calloused fingertips roamed down the curve of my ass. There was something about him that made the rest of the world disappear. It was just him and me, and nothing else mattered. A soft whimper escaped my lips as he deepened the kiss. Water cascaded down our bodies as he lowered his hands to my thighs and lifted me, pressing my back against the cold, wet tile. Seeking more, I released his mouth and tilted my head back, letting the water flow down my breasts. He trailed kisses along the curves of my neck to my collarbone, and ever so slowly, he moved his hand up and down my slick side. His fingers brushed against my breasts down to my hips, and I groaned with pleasure as his hand found its way between my legs. His fingers slipped inside me, moving ever so gently as he whispered, "You don't know what you do to me."

"Tell me," I gasped as he moved faster inside me.

"I haven't been able to get you out of my head...."

I've been thinking about all the things I'm going to do to you, and all the ways I'm going to make you come. You're mine... all of you."

Hearing him say the words sent me over the edge. My hips jerked forward as my body clenched firmly around his fingers. I was floating on the high of my release, relishing the moment of bliss, when I felt him lower me to my feet. With my eyes still closed in a haze of pleasure, I hadn't even noticed that he'd lowered himself down to his knees before me. His mouth came closer, and with one flick of his tongue, my hips jolted forward. My hands dove into his hair as I shamelessly pulled him closer. My body went into complete sensory overload, and he had just gotten started. What began in the shower moved into the bedroom, where he spent the entire night exploring every inch of my body.

By the time he was done, we were both exhausted and wondrously sated and collapsed on the bed. He laid his head on the pillow as I curled into his side, resting my head on the crook of his arm. We lay there motionless for several minutes, trying to catch our breath. I'm not sure what spurred the thought, maybe it was feeling the connection between us growing, or maybe I just needed him to know. Either way, I looked up at him. "Nathan?"

"Um hmm."

I propped up on my elbow, so I could look at him as I said, "When my parents were killed in that car crash, I was worried I'd never find real happiness again.

I was young, and they meant everything to me. I thought my chances of a good life died with them." I took in a deep breath and slowly exhaled before I continued, "I had some good days, but they were never enough. When those people took me and tried to sell me off to some stranger... I thought I'd run out of chances, but then there you were."

His voice was soft and low as he whispered, "Tristen."

"I just wanted to tell you, I'm happy... really happy, and it's all because of you."

He didn't respond. I didn't expect him to. He told me he'd tell me what had happened to him, and I trusted that he would when he got ready. I closed my eyes as I listened to the relaxing rhythm of his heartbeat, and even though I tried to fight it, I drifted off to sleep. I woke up the next morning in an empty bed with a note from Nathan on my pillow letting me know he'd gone to work. I was disappointed, but not surprised, as I crawled out of bed and headed to the shower. By the time I was out and dressed, it was almost noon, and I was starving. With my stomach growling, I headed towards the kitchen. When I got to the refrigerator, I found another note. It was from Max. He'd gone down to one of the other apartments to take care of something.

I'd just finished making a bowl of some healthy, multi-grain cereal when Max walked in sporting the same serious expression he'd been wearing all week. Getting right down to business, he asked, "Are you working today?"

"Nope. I have the next two days off, but I have a few errands I need to run."

"What kind of errands?"

"I need to go by the bank, and then over to the college… and maybe by the mall."

"The mall?" he groaned.

"I'll be fast. I promise." I put my bowl of uneaten cereal in the sink and started for my room. "Oh, and we'll need to stop for lunch!"

"Cereal not your thing?"

"Not that kind of cereal. It's awful, like something my grandmother might eat if she was constipated."

I could hear him chuckling as I walked into my room and grabbed my purse. When I came back out, he asked, "Where to first?"

"The bank, and then you pick where we go to eat -- preferably a place without rabbit food."

"I think we can manage that."

After I deposited my paycheck, Max took us to a diner in town for a cheeseburger and fries. Once we were done, he drove me over to the college campus, so I could finalize my enrollment. After I got all that sorted, we got back in the car and headed towards the mall. "Do you have any idea how long it's been since I've been inside a mall?"

"That long?"

"I was probably seventeen, and I'd only gone because I had to. My sister wouldn't stop nagging me to take her and some of her friends. I had no idea what I was getting myself into. Those girls were out of their minds. They had no rhyme or reason to anything. They went into every damn store and tried on every fucking thing they had, and I had to sit there and watch. It was not my idea of a good afternoon."

The wide-eyed, goofy expression on his face made me laugh, but not the cute giggle kind of laugh. I let loose an obnoxiously loud, and apparently contagious, guffaw. When he heard me snort, Max started in, and in a matter of seconds, we were both laughing hysterically over nothing. Once we'd caught our breath, I looked over to him and said, "Why didn't you just go to the men's section or something?"

"I couldn't leave them. My sister was just eleven or twelve at the time, and I figured I needed to keep an eye on them. Besides, my mom would've had my hide if something had happened to them."

"That was sweet, Max. You were a good brother."

"I'm not so sure Anna Kate would agree with you on that. I could be a real pain in the ass."

"You? Surely not." I smiled. "Do you have any other brothers or sisters?"

"No. Just Anna Kate, but she was enough. Trust me."

The last few times I'd seen Max, he'd seemed preoccupied and worried, so it was good to finally see him smiling. I liked the more laidback version of him, so I decided to resist the urge to ask him what had been bothering him. Once he'd parked the car in front of the mall, he reluctantly followed me inside. As promised, I tried to make the trip as painless as possible, but it wasn't easy. Each store brought new ideas, making me want to expand my wardrobe even more. I tried to limit my shopping to just some new jeans and shirts, but I found myself wishing I had time to check out the other things on display.

"I'm sorry, Max." I told him as I rushed into my favorite store. "I'll try to hurry."

"You're fine," he groaned. I grabbed a few jeans and headed into the dressing room. I'd only tried on the first pair when Max called out to me. "We need to go."

"Why? Is something wrong?"

"No."

"Then why do we need to rush off?"

"Nitro wants me to bring you over to his mother's place."

I stuck my head out of the dressing room, and my voice rose several octaves higher as I asked, "His mother's? Why?"

"He didn't say."

"Okay. Give me two minutes." Trying to contain my panic, I closed the door and took a deep breath. Meeting his parents was a huge step. I knew things with Nathan had taken a turn, but I didn't think we'd reached that definitive point in our relationship. My heart pounded with nerves as I took off the new jeans and changed back into my clothes. As I took the pants up to the cashier, I looked over to Max, "You think everything's okay?"

"Everything is fine. You'll like Clara." As soon as I'd checked out, I followed Max to his car.

My mind raced as we drove out onto the main road. It was a short trip, and I hadn't had time to truly prepare myself before Max pulled into the assisted living complex. Nathan was waiting for us out front and watched as Max parked the car next to him. As soon as I got out, he gave a quick nod to Nathan and pulled off, leaving me and my overactive nerves behind. Nathan reached for my hand and led me up to the front door. Before he opened it, I gave his arm a quick tug. "What are we doing here?"

"Just checking in on her."

"And you suddenly thought it would be a good idea to bring me along?"

A mischievous smile spread across his face as he answered, "Yep."

"*Nathan.*"

Before I had a chance to protest any further, he opened the door and shouted, "Mom?"

"Come on in, sweetheart. I'm in the living room." We stepped inside a quaint little kitchen with tall white cabinets and pale, sage green walls. The fresh scent of chocolate chip cookies lingered in the air as we continued into the living room. His mother's eyes lit up as she saw us coming through the doorway. She came over to Nathan with a big smile on her face and her arms opened wide. "Why didn't you tell me you were coming by? I would've fixed dinner."

"That's exactly why I didn't tell you," he told her as he hugged her.

She smiled as she turned her attention to me. "And you brought company."

"I did," he smiled. "I'd like you to meet Tristen."

"She's beautiful, Nate." Her eyes were blue like her son's, but that was the only similarity I could see. She was a petite little thing, barely coming up to my shoulders, and her hair was short and full of beautiful, wavy curls. As if she already knew me, she reached for me, hugging me tightly as she said, "It's so good to meet you, Tristen. You can call me Clara."

"It's nice to meet you, too, Clara."

"What a nice surprise. I can't remember the last time Nathan brought a friend—"

"You want something to drink?" Nathan interrupted. "Coffee or some tea?"

"I just made a pot of tea."

"I'll get you a cup."

"Come have a seat, Tristen." I followed Clara over to the sofa and sat down next to her. "Tell me a little something about yourself."

"There's not much to tell really," I answered as Nathan returned and placed the cup next to her.

"Nathan, don't you think you should offer Tristen something to drink as well?"

A boyish grin crossed his face as he turned and

looked at me. "Can I get you something?"

"Sure. A cup of tea would be great."

"You got it."

I was amused as I watched the big, self-assured man scurry off to the kitchen to fetch my cup of tea, and I couldn't help but smile.

He came back in the room, and after he placed my cup on the table, he sat down next to me. "Thank you."

Nathan looked over at his mother and asked, "Has Colton gone back?"

"Yes, they left early this morning. He seemed really happy, don't you think?"

"He did."

"I'm glad you were able to spend some time with him."

Nathan's expression was less than sincere as he answered, "Me, too."

As they chattered back and forth, I looked around at all the pictures on the walls and side tables, seeing Nathan's childhood displayed across the room. I picked up one of the pictures of him with an older man and smiled. "This is such a great picture. Is this Nathan's father?"

"It is. That was taken at his high school graduation."

"I'm sure he's pleased with how well Nathan is doing."

"Yes, dear. I'm sure he would be very proud if he were still with us, but... I like to think he's still watching over us. Our own guardian angel."

"Oh, I'm sorry. I didn't realize," I replied as I looked over at Nathan.

"Nathaniel James." Her voice was full of surprise as she turned and looked at her son. The air suddenly felt heavy as she said, "You haven't told her?"

Chapter 13
Nitro

Murray and Mom had tried a thousand times to get me to talk about it, but I'd never opened up to anyone about what had happened that night. I didn't see the point. I knew there was no way they could even begin to comprehend what it felt like to lose the girl that held my heart in her hand, to have my little daughter ripped away from me before I'd even had a chance to hold her in my arms, and to have my father taken from me when I needed him the most. In one fell swoop, they were all taken from me. No one could know the guilt that weighed on me, so I carried the pain on my own. I kept it locked away, hoping that one day I might be able to forget, but deep down, I knew it would never happen. It had become part of me, rooted deep down in my bones. It had changed me, making me hard and bitter. I'd hurt the people that cared about me the most. I'd shut them out and refused to let them get close. I was broken, but I was still standing. The demons of my past hadn't won yet. Each moment I spent with Tristen, the stronger I became. She made me feel like I could move forward, beyond the heartache and guilt. I could have a second chance, an opportunity for redemption, and I wanted it. I wanted it with her.

She hadn't spoken to me since we'd left my

mother's. As soon as we got home, she changed and got into bed, turning away from my side as she curled into her pillow. When I lay down next to her, she didn't budge. She was upset with me, and I couldn't say that I blamed her. I wasn't sure how long we lay there in silence, but I could tell from the heavy rhythm of her breathing that she wasn't asleep. I rolled towards her, spooning into her back with my mouth close to her ear. "I was twenty-two when it happened."

I slipped my arm around her waist as I continued, "I was just a stupid kid. I thought I had it all figured out, that nothing could stand in my way, but I couldn't have been more wrong."

Her back stiffened as I said, "Lainey meant everything to me. We were high school sweethearts of all things, but what we had wasn't your typical teenage romance. It was real, and it was good. She was pregnant, about eight months along. We were having a little girl... Lila Grace." My voice strained as I said her name. It felt like a lifetime since I'd said it aloud. I wanted Tristen to know how much my unborn child meant to me, but there was no way I could put it into words. "I remember the day we went for the ultrasound. I can still see the profile of her little face with her thumb in her mouth. It was the most beautiful sight I'd ever seen. We'd planned our future together: marriage, a house in the mountains, and two or three kids... but we never got the chance."

Trying to ground myself, I toyed with the ends of

her hair, reminding myself that she was right there, and I took a deep, cleansing breath. I didn't want to say the words. I'd kept it bottled up for so long, and saying it out loud made it all seem too real. "There was nothing really special about that night. We'd gone to eat at my parents'. It was just like many times before. Mom had fixed one of her big dinners, but she needed something from the store, so I offered to go for her. I was only gone for a few minutes…."

Sensing that I was struggling, she rolled over to face me, placing her hand on my chest. "Just breathe."

I paused for a moment, collecting my thoughts before I continued. "The second I walked through the door I knew something was wrong. I felt it. When I walked into the living room, I saw them there. It didn't seem real, like it was just some awful fucking dream."

"What happened?"

"While I was gone, someone broke into the house. Lainey… my little Lila Grace… my father, someone had shot them all. They'd left them to die like they were nothing more than garbage. Mom was the only one that survived, but it took her months to recover."

"Oh my god, Nathan," she cried, tears streaming down her face. "Oh my god. That's so awful. It's too horrible to imagine."

"They meant everything to me."

She ran the tips of her fingers across my chest and down my arm as she whispered, "I'm so, so sorry, Nathan."

"I lost everything that day, and it's all my fault. I should've been there. I should've done something. I was supposed to protect them, but I wasn't there when they needed me."

"But you can't blame yourself. There's no way you could've known what was going to happen."

"I'd overheard my father talking to the men. I knew in my gut something wasn't right, but...."

"It's not your fault, Nathan. I think deep down you know that." She rested her hand on my shoulder as she told me, "When my parents died, I was so angry. I couldn't understand why I had to be the one who lost my family. I kept trying to think of what I'd done to deserve something so horrible to happen to me. Over time, the anger started to fade, and the guilt crept in. I didn't think it was fair for me to still be alive when they were dead."

"It's not fair. I shouldn't be here living when they're stuck in that fucking grave. It should've been me."

"No, Nathan. You're wrong. It took a long time, but I finally realized...." She raised up, her hand on my chest and her face just inches from mine as she said, "No amount of guilt is going to change the past, Nathan."

With that, she lowered herself into the crook of my arm and rested her head on my chest. I let her words sink in, letting them roll around in my mind as the warmth of her skin next to mine calmed the storm of emotions raging inside me. We lay there quietly for several minutes before I kissed her on her forehead and said, "I should've told you sooner."

"Yes, but I understand why you didn't. I wish there was something I could do."

"Don't you know? You already have."

After several moments of silence, she looked up at me and said, "Will you tell me something about her?"

Her question caught me off guard. I hadn't really talked about Lainey in years. It was just too hard, but thinking about her then, I smiled. "She was the funniest person I'd ever met. She could make you laugh without even trying." Tristen rested the palm of her hand on my chest as her body relaxed next to mine. "There was something about her smile that could make you forget everything around you... but she was also strong and determined as hell. When she set her mind to something, there was nothing that could stop her, especially when it came to me. She never let me get away with any of my bullshit."

"I bet that wasn't easy."

"You have no idea." I laughed. "I thought I knew it all, but she managed to keep me grounded the best she could. She was beautiful... even more so when she was pregnant. I've never seen anyone so excited about having a kid. She had the nursery decked out and all these baby clothes.... She had everything you could imagine." My chest tightened, and my voice became strained as I said, "She would've been an amazing mother."

Several minutes passed, and neither of us spoke. Realizing that I'd probably said too much, I looked down at her and said, "I'm sorry for laying all that on you."

"Don't be. I'm glad you loved her that deeply, Nathan. It means you're capable of a love like that... so maybe there's hope for me yet."

There was no more talking, no making love—just us lying next to one another as we let the silence of the night envelope us. The tightness in my chest started to fade, and with her tucked at my side, I finally drifted off to sleep. The next morning, I woke up with Tristen draped over me. She had one leg over mine, and her head plastered against my chest. She looked absolutely stunning, and I hated to disturb her, but my bladder wasn't going to let me lie there another minute. I tried to ease out of the bed without waking her. Unfortunately, that didn't happen. As soon as I tried to move her onto the pillow, her eyes popped open. She looked up at me and smiled. "Hey."

"Morning, Angel." I kissed her gently on the lips before getting out of bed.

She raised up on her elbow and watched as I walked into the bathroom. "Did you sleep okay?"

"I did. You?"

"Like a rock." She'd gotten out of bed and was looking at her phone when I walked back into the room. "You have any plans for this afternoon?"

"I've got a little work to take care of, but it shouldn't take long. Do you have something in mind?"

"I'm going over to check on Josie for a little while. You want to hang out after? Maybe grab some dinner or something? I mean... if you have time."

I walked over and kissed her on the temple. "I'll make time."

"Great."

"If you want, I'll drop you off on my way to the office."

"That would be perfect. I've got to take a quick shower." She started for the door but stopped in her tracks. She turned to face me with sincerity in her eyes. "I'm glad we talked last night."

"Me, too."

Her lips curled into a smile as she turned to leave. "Okay, I'll be back in a few." Half an hour later, she came into the kitchen looking beautiful with her jeans and pullover V-neck shirt. Her hair was down around her shoulders, wavy and dark, and she'd put on just a touch of makeup and silver earrings. "Ready when you are."

We got in the car and headed over to Big's. It had been a while since the last time I'd been out to his place, but the minute I pulled up in the driveway, I could tell that Josie was making her mark. From the bright colored flowers lining the walkway to the pansies in the window boxes, she had turned his house into a home. I stopped the car and turned to Tristen. "Call Max and let him know when you're ready to come home."

"I can get Josie to run me back." I gave her a stern look, and she shook her head. "Okay. Okay. I'll call him."

"Have fun, and tell Josie I said hello."

She got out and smiled. "You know I will."

I was about to pull out of the driveway, when Big came out onto the front porch. He was a big guy, not at all what you'd think a computer hacker might look like, but he was the best around. We'd formed an unlikely friendship during our stint in prison. I'd gotten word that Lenny DeMarco had been locked up, and I'd thought it was my chance to finally get my hands on him. To most people it probably seemed like an asinine thing to do, but back then, I had nothing to lose and everything to gain by going to prison. I'd figured that while I was there I could expand my father's business. I could make some new connections and build trust among the inmates. It was the best way I knew to get my name out there and prove that I could follow in my father's footsteps. When I'd crossed paths with Big, I knew from the start that he'd be an asset, and I couldn't have been more right. Over the years, he'd saved my ass on more than one occasion, and I owed him my life for always having my back. Until it was gone, I hadn't realized how valuable my ties with him had really been.

I watched as he slowly made his way to my SUV. It'd been several weeks since I'd come face to face with him at the clubhouse, and I wasn't sure how things would play out as I opened my door and stepped out. "How's it going?"

"Good. You know how it is. Never a dull moment."

I motioned my head towards the flowers on the front steps. "Looks like Josie is settling in."

"She is." He turned back towards the house as he said, "Tristen looks better. *Much better*."

"That was the plan all along."

"Guess things worked out after all. See ya around, Nitro," he clipped as he started towards his bike.

"Hey, Big."

"Yeah?" He stopped and glared at me.

"I'm not a man who likes to admit when he's wrong."

Big scoffed, "No news flash there, brother."

"I should've handled things differently. I owed you more than that."

"Yeah, well the club…" he started.

"I'm not talking about the club, brother. Just you." Big was a good man. He may not have agreed with the way I handled things with the club, but I knew in time he'd see that I'd done it for Tristen.

"Appreciate that." He looked over his shoulder towards the house. "You know… Josie is going to wanna see Tristen. *A lot*. You know how sisters can be."

"I do."

"Guess I'll be seeing you around."

I smiled. "I guess you will."

He didn't have to say the words. I knew what he

was saying. I gave him a quick nod as I slipped back inside my SUV and pulled out of the driveway. When I got to the office, Murray and Ryder were there waiting for me. Ryder was leaned back in the chair smoking a cigarette, while Murray was talking on the phone. He was just hanging up when I sat down at my desk. "What's the latest?"

Ryder sat up in his seat as he explained, "The load was dropped. Thirty-two thousand tons of timber and the shipment were lost at sea, but no issues with the Coast Guard."

"Good to hear."

Murray looked over to me and said, "We're going to have to move some things around to get these orders out on time."

"I talked to Tate. He's bringing his delivery in early."

"I'll put a call into Reedy and see if he can do the same." I turned to Ryder and told him, "Gonna need you tomorrow. I've got a meet in California, and I'm going to need you to tag along."

"You got it, boss," Ryder answered as he stood up to leave.

Just as he walked out, my phone chimed with a text message.

Tristen:

Hey

Damaged Goods

Me:

Everything okay?

Tristen:

Yeah. Just wanted to say hi.

Me:

Missing me already?

Tristen:

Maybe a little.

Me:

A little?

Tristen:

Okay. More than a little.

Me:

Good to hear. See you soon, Angel.

"What the hell was that all about?" Murray mocked.

"What?"

"You're fucking smiling."

"And?"

"It's good to see it. Just wondering why."

"I guess you could say that things are looking up."

"Well, it's about fucking time."

Things *were* looking up. For the first time in years, I felt lighter, like the world wasn't weighing down on my shoulders. Without even realizing she was doing it, Tristen had taken some of the load off, and I found myself wanting to do something special for her. I remembered Max telling me that Tristen had asked him to take her to the mall. I'd cut the trip short when I told him to bring her over to Mom's. I sent Max a message, telling him to get in touch with a lady friend of his. Tristen deserved the very best, and I was going to make damn well sure she got it.

Chapter 14
Tristen

"This place is really something," I told Josie as I followed her into the kitchen. We all knew Big had a place of his own, but he spent most of his time at the club, mainly because he was always working on something. Since I was just one of the girls working at the club, I never really knew what was going on. None of the girls had, not even the ol' ladies. Club business was never something we talked about, but we all knew Big played an important role. With his special set of skills, he was able to find things out that no one else could. "Are you liking it here?"

"I love it. I thought I'd get lonely being all the way out here, but between finishing up school and spending time at the club, we're always on the go."

"I'll have to admit, I never thought I'd see the day when my big sister would hook up with a biker."

"You and me both." She laughed. "But he makes me really happy."

"I can tell." I sat down at the counter and took a drink of my sweet tea. "Not to freak you out or anything, but Big has always reminded me a little of Dad."

"What? Do not put a thought like that in my head!"

"Seriously, he does. It's not his looks or anything. I

mean, come on. Big is hot, but with all that computer stuff, he's really smart, and he's good at what he does."

"He's got the gift."

"But you do, too. I heard about you hacking the club."

"Yeah, well, that's probably not the smartest thing I've ever done."

"Maybe not, but it all turned out really good. Look at you. You've got the man of your dreams, a beautiful home, and you're about to graduate college. Mom and Dad would've been so proud."

She walked over and gave me a tight hug. "They would be proud of you, too. I hope you know that."

"I'm not so sure."

"You've come a long way, Tris. You've got a great job, you've already been promoted, and you're starting college in a few weeks."

"I haven't exactly done it all on my own."

"And neither did I. We all need some help from time to time." She gave me a look as she asked, "So, how are things with you and Nitro?"

"It's complicated." I spent the next few minutes telling her about what had happened to Nathan. I didn't go into all the sordid details. I just told her enough for her to understand why things weren't exactly easy. I immediately regretted telling her, though, when I saw the expression on her face. "It's fine, Josie."

"I don't know. Something like that messes you up in ways that no one really understands."

"Maybe, but if you can find your way through it, then you come back stronger."

"But if you don't, then you're screwed up for life."

"I never thought of you as the negative type. Here you are with a biker who's a freaking computer hacker. If you can put a positive spin on that, then you can put it on anything."

"That's different. Big loves me. He really loves me. I'd just hate to see you fall for someone who won't be able to love you the way you deserve."

"Well, it's too late for that. I'm already falling for him."

She sighed as she replied, "I know. I could tell the minute you walked through the door. Just don't lose yourself in this guy. If he can't be the man you need him to be, and I mean in every way, then walk away."

"It wouldn't be easy to walk away from Nathan."

"No, I imagine it wouldn't be. Hopefully, it won't come to that." She walked over to the refrigerator and looked inside. "On a different note, how about a sandwich? We could eat it out on the porch."

"That sounds great. Need some help?"

"I've got it. I know how you tend to overdo it with the mayonnaise."

"The more mayo the better."

"Ugh," she laughed. "Why don't you just refill our drinks?"

"I can do that."

Josie started making our sandwiches while I

grabbed the pitcher of tea. I'd just finished refilling our glasses when she asked, "You didn't tell me which classes you signed up for."

"I'm just starting with the basics for now. With work, I'll only be able to take a few at a time."

"Why don't you just use the money that Mom and Dad...."

"I don't want to do that," I interrupted. "I know it may sound crazy to you, but I need to do this on my own."

"It does sound crazy, Tristen. They left us that money so they could secure our future."

"I'm sure that money will come in handy at some point, but for now, I need to do this my way, Josie."

"You've always been so stubborn."

"And you haven't?" I teased.

"I guess that's one trait we got from Mom. Stubborn as the day is long."

"I think you have a lot of Mom in you."

"Oh, really? Like what?"

"Her smile for one... and her heart. You've always had a way of seeing the best in people."

"That's not always a good thing."

"It is a good thing. A very good thing." She finished up the sandwiches and said, "You ready to eat?"

"Absolutely."

We spent the next hour out on the porch, talking and catching up. She told me all about Lauren and how well she was doing with Cass and Cotton. Lauren was a special young girl, and it did my heart good to know that she was truly doing well. When it came time for Josie to go to school, I sent Max a message letting him know I was ready for him to come get me. Once I'd finished helping her take our dishes back into the kitchen, I turned to her and asked, "Do you think there will ever come a time when we can all have dinner together or something?"

"What do you mean?"

"With everything that happened with Nathan and the club... do you think they'll ever be able to move past it?"

"I'd like to think so, but you never know. Sometimes men can be bullheaded. Let's just give it some time and see how things play out."

As much as I enjoyed my visit with my sister, I left there feeling a little out of sorts. She had me thinking about the future, especially my future with Nathan, and I found myself wondering if maybe she was right. Maybe a past like Nathan's was just too hard to overcome. Maybe he wouldn't ever be able to love me the way I wanted him to, but that didn't mean I wasn't going to give him a chance. I wanted a future with him, a chance to find a place in his heart, and I just had to hold on to the hope that I might actually have it one day.

"You okay over there? Looks like you have something on your mind," Max asked, pulling me from my thoughts.

"Oh, sorry. I was just in my own world there for a minute. Everything's fine."

"Good. You had me worried for a minute."

"Can I ask you something?"

"Sure."

"Do you have someone special in your life? You know, like a girlfriend or something?"

"No. I can't say that I do."

"Why not?"

"I don't have time for it." He shrugged his shoulders. "I have my fun, but when it comes down to it, something real just isn't in the cards for me."

"I'm sure if the right girl came along, you'd see things differently."

"I already found the right girl, but like I said, something real just isn't in the cards for me."

"But, how do…."

"I'm good, Tristen. I like the way things are. No need in complicating things."

"Okay, I'll leave it, but you should think about it. Sometimes the complications are what makes life worthwhile."

After Max dropped me off, I decided to take a hot bath and change my clothes, so I would be ready when Nathan got home. Before I started the water, I went to the closet to find something to wear. When I opened the door, I was surprised to find that it was filled with extravagant dresses, shirts, and pants. I was taken aback as I took out one of the long, black dresses. I held it up to my chest as I looked in the mirror. I loved how the A-line flowed at the hips. It was absolutely stunning. Excitement surged through me as I rushed over to the closet and reached for another dress, and then another and another. Each one of them was simply amazing. When I came across a little black dress with a low cut back, I quickly undressed and slipped it on. The fabric hung perfectly against my body, like it was made for me, and I'd never felt so beautiful.

Deciding that it would be the perfect outfit for my night with Nathan, I took it off and laid it across the bed. I went over to my dresser and found each drawer filled to the brim with new jeans, t-shirts, bras, and panties. I was sifting through the new clothes when it hit me. An awful feeling crept over me as I realized my things weren't there—none of them. Panic rushed through me as I frantically pulled everything out of the drawers, piling the t-shirts, jeans, and undergarments onto the floor. I searched for something-- anything-- that was mine. I checked and checked again, but they were gone. What had started out as every girl's fantasy had turned into an absolute nightmare. I got up and searched the closet, and again found nothing of mine. I raced around the room as I checked every drawer and every cabinet. Finding no sign of them, I checked the other rooms. Nothing.

I was devastated. It was one thing to buy a girl a few new things, to try to make her feel special, but this was something else altogether. He'd taken what was mine and tossed it out like last week's trash. I stood there staring at the new clothes piled on the floor, and I felt absolutely heartbroken. I couldn't understand why he'd done it. I felt like the walls were closing in on me, so I slipped on my bathrobe and went into the living room. As I sat on the sofa, my anger continued to boil inside of me. By the time Nathan walked through the door, I was beyond furious with him. I turned and glared at him as he tossed his keys on the counter and started over to me. "What have you *done*?"

He cocked his head in confusion. "What's wrong?"

"The clothes, Nathan."

"Ah, that's right. The new clothes." He smiled as he sat down next to me. "Do you like them?"

I was trying to stay calm, but it wasn't easy, especially with that damn smile on his face. "Where are my things?"

"What are you so upset about? You have new things. Everything you could possibly need."

"Maybe I didn't want all *new things*, Nathan. Did you ever think of that? No, of course you didn't." I stood up and started to pace. "You are so damn frustrating!"

"I didn't…" he started.

"You just do whatever you think is best, and go with it, to hell with what anyone else wants! You can't do that. It's not right!"

"I was trying to do something good here."

"There is nothing good about taking someone's

things without telling them. It's intrusive and just… stupid!" I stopped and crossed my arms as I turned to face him. "Just tell me what you've done with my things."

"I thought you'd like…" he began.

"You thought I'd like to have my things thrown out and replaced with all new stuff? Well, you couldn't have been more wrong! They are *my* things, not yours!"

"Hold on a minute." He stood up and walked over to me, placing his hands on my hips as he tried to calm me down. "I was trying to do something good here, Angel."

"This goes back to you thinking that I'm a possession, that you can just go into my room and take my things without even talking to me about it. It's scary that you think you have that kind of control over me, Nathan. I know you were trying to do a good thing, but that only makes it more frightening." I placed my hand on his chest as I continued, "What if the tables were turned, and I'd gone into your room, taken your things, and replaced them all with things I liked? How would you feel?"

"I get that I messed up, but you have to give me a chance to fix it."

Seeing that he was genuinely concerned, I let out a deep breath. "My dad's t-shirt. It's the *only* thing I have of his. I wear it whenever I'm feeling homesick or out of place. It means a lot to me."

"I'll get it back. No matter what it takes, I'll get it

all back, Angel." He pulled me close, hugging me tightly as he kissed me on the temple. "I wasn't thinking."

"I really love the clothes, Nathan. It's just...."

"I know. I fucked up." He pulled his phone out of his side pocket and sent a message to someone. When they answered back, he turned and started for the door. "I'll be right back."

"Where are you going?"

"Just sit tight. I won't be long."

I tried to be patient, but after thirty minutes had passed, I began to wonder if something was wrong, or if my things would be lost forever. Just as I was about to go look for him, the door opened, and he stepped inside carrying two large bags. "I think this is all of it."

I rushed over to him and took one of the bags from his hand. I quickly opened it and was relieved to see my things were inside. "Oh, thank god. They're all here!"

He didn't respond as I continued to rifle through the bag. When I finally stood up and actually looked at him, I saw that his shirt and pants were filthy and stained, and he smelled bad, really bad. "Wait a minute. What happened to you?"

"Let's not talk about it." He smiled and started walking down the hall. "I'm going to take a shower. When I get out, I'll help you get your things back where they belong."

"That's not necessary. I can do it."

He stopped, and when he turned to look at me, I

immediately regretted being so angry with him. "As far as the new stuff goes, keep what you want, and toss the rest. I didn't mean…."

I walked over to him, wrapping my arms around his neck as I said, "I really do love the new clothes, but… Nathan, you have to be willing to take the risk to love and know that you might lose. You can't control every little thing that happens to the people you care about, no matter how much you love them or want to keep them safe."

"You're right, but… I'm trying here, Tristen." He looked at me with such emotion in his eyes that it made my heart ache for him. "I know I have a lot to learn about all this stuff. You're gonna have to teach me."

Hearing those words tugged at my heart. His sincerity was just another reason that I found myself falling for him even more. I lifted up on my tiptoes, pressing my lips against his in a kiss, then I said, "We'll learn together."

With that, he took my hand and led me down the hall. We never left the house that night. Instead, we took a long, hot shower together and spent the night in bed, making love, and holding each other close. I lay there feeling like I'd made some real progress with him. We'd had our first argument, and he'd actually listened when I talked to him. I thought we might have a real chance after all. I fell asleep with a smile on my face, happy and content in Nathan's arms. The next morning, I woke to find Nathan shuffling around the room. He was buttoning his white collared shirt when I sat up in the bed and asked, "What time is it?"

"It's early, Angel. Go back to sleep."

Just as I was about to lay back down, I noticed his black, duffle bag sitting on the floor. "Are you going somewhere?"

"I've got to go out of town for the day, but I'm planning to be back later tonight." He walked over to the bed, then leaned over to kiss me. "If you need anything, Max will be around. Just let him know whatever you need."

He started for the door, but stopped when I called out to him. "Nathan?" When he turned to face me, I wanted to tell him that I loved him, that I'd never felt that way before, but I couldn't form the words. I don't know what stopped me. Maybe it was the fear of scaring him off or finally admitting my feelings out loud. Either way, the risk was just too great. For the moment, I had to keep my feelings to myself. "Have a safe trip."

Chapter 15
Nitro

You never know how damaged you are until you try to share your life with another person. I'd lived in my own world, by my own rules, and I'd never given a fuck who I hurt in the process. It's who I was, but when I saw the anguish on Tristen's face, when I realized I'd hurt her, it was like a knife to the chest. There was nothing I wouldn't do to fix it, even if that meant diving into a fucking dumpster to go after her stuff. Thankfully, I found her things and managed to smooth things over, but the whole episode left me with an unsettling feeling. I started to think that I was too screwed up to make things work with her. I'd thought if I protected her and cared for her, gave her everything she could possibly want, it would be enough, but it wasn't. It was going to take more, much more, and I wasn't sure I had it to give.

For the time being, though, I had to put my doubts aside and focus on the day ahead. Ryder and I were on the plane headed to California, and I was feeling a little uneasy. I'd never been a fan of flying. Being cooped up in a little space almost 40,000 feet up in the air just wasn't exactly appealing to me. I looked over to Ryder sprawled out in his chair, eyes closed and completely relaxed, and I felt a tinge of jealousy. While he looked happy as a fucking lark, I was wound tight as a drum, and I just wanted to get the hell off that plane. I reached for a magazine, hoping it might distract me, and started thumbing through the pages. It didn't work, and I grew more tense by the minute.

Without opening his eyes, Ryder asked, "You doing okay over there, boss?"

"Doing just fine, asshole."

"Just checking. You look a little stiff."

"I said I was fine, smartass."

"Good." He turned and looked at me as he asked, "You reckon we could talk about the plan for today?"

"We've got the meet with Dayton."

"Whatcha think of this guy?"

"I have my doubts about tying up with him."

"Any reason why?"

"Just got a feeling. I'll know more after we have a face to face."

"Where are you meeting this guy?"

"A restaurant out south. We'll need to get there early. I want eyes on him the minute he shows up."

"You got it." He leaned his head back against the chair and closed his eyes. "Give me a heads up when we get there."

The motherfucker slept the rest of the flight and even through the landing. Once the plane had stopped, I gave him a quick jab with my elbow and said, "We're here."

With a quick nod, he grabbed our bags from the

overhead compartment and headed off the plane. I'd called ahead and arranged for us to have a rental for the drive over to the restaurant. I went over to the desk and got the keys, and Ryder followed me out to the SUV. He put our luggage in the back and got in the driver's seat. "Where to, boss?"

"Head out on the interstate. We'll need to go to the south end of Sacramento." I leaned back and closed my eyes. "It's about ten minutes from here. Let me know when we get close."

"Hold up. What's the name of the restaurant?"

"The Firehouse."

"Okay. I think I know the place."

With all the traffic and Ryder's inability to follow the GPS, the drive took longer than expected. We were still relatively early, giving us both time to give the place a once over. It was an old fire station that they'd converted into a restaurant, and over the years it had become a hot spot in the area. I'd been there a time or two before and knew you could choose to eat out in the courtyard or in one of the many different dining rooms. I opted to sit in the bar. It had the best view of the entire restaurant, so I would be able to see Dayton the moment he walked in. I'd reserved a table in one of the smaller dining rooms and left word with the maître d' to have him wait for me at the table. That would give me a chance to check him out before I actually approached him.

I'd just finished my gin and tonic when Ryder sent

me a text message letting me know that Dayton had arrived. When Dayton stepped through the door, I immediately recognized him from the picture in his file. He was much shorter than me, about five-seven and as round as he was tall. Even though it was nearly ninety degrees outside, he was wearing a black suit with his coat buttoned, trying to hide his large gut. His thinning hair was combed to the side, and his goatee came to a point at the end of his chin. He looked like a younger, Californian-version of Colonel Sanders as one of the waiters led him over to our table. His three men, who were also wearing dark suits, dispersed throughout the room, but they didn't go far. Each of them was standing close by in case something went wrong. The guy was playing it smart, which was a good sign, but it hadn't eased my doubts about him. I waited until he'd ordered a drink before I walked over to the table and sat down.

He gave me the once over and then snickered, "You must be the infamous Mr. Nitro."

"Nitro will suffice."

"Well, it's an honor to finally meet you. I've heard many great things about you."

I knew he was just blowing smoke up my ass, so I asked, "Such as?"

"Well, things like… you're a man who gets the job done. You don't cut corners, and you're dependable. I've been told you're the best around."

"And *who* exactly told you that?"

"My man, Nix. We've worked together for years.

Well… we did until recently. As I told you on the phone, he is no longer in the business."

"I assume that he didn't have a choice in the matter."

"No. I guess he didn't," he said as he motioned for the waiter. As soon as he arrived, Dayton ordered. "I'll have the vande rose pork chop with extra butter on the potatoes, and he'll have…."

"Nothing. Thank you."

"Suit yourself." He took a sip of his bourbon and then continued without skipping a beat. "Unfortunately, Nix ran into a little trouble. That's why I contacted you. I was hoping you might be able to take up the slack."

I had no idea why, but my gut told me there was something off about the guy. Maybe it was his pompous attitude, or the way his lips curled into an evil grin whenever he spoke, but something told me it was time to walk away from the asshole. "That's not going to happen."

"What the hell are you talking about?"

"I'm not doing business with you, Mr. Dayton."

"But why?"

"*Why…* isn't important."

"You little piece of shit." His face grew red and the veins in his fat neck started to bulge as he shouted, "You don't know who you're dealing with!"

"You're wrong. I know exactly who you are, Jim Dayton. I know your guy just got put away for twenty years because you fucked up."

"You don't know what you're talking about."

"I know this: there are no second chances in this game, and as far as you are concerned, I'm done." As I looked over my shoulder I noticed one of his guys moving in our direction. I stood up and glared at him. "Tread lightly, Dayton. You don't want the kind of blowback I can throw at you. Cut your losses and move on."

"You're going to regret this."

"I doubt it, but only time will tell." I walked off, leaving him to stew angrily as I made my way over to Ryder.

"You done?"

"Past done. Let's get the hell out of here." I was on edge as I followed Ryder out to the truck. Gaining new clients was part of the process, but it was always risky. You never knew how things would play out, but something told me I'd made the right decision walking away from Dayton. It was only a matter of time before that motherfucker ended up on the five o'clock news or dead, and I wanted no part of it.

When we got in the truck, Ryder looked down at his watch. "We've got some time to kill. You up for grabbing some lunch? I'm starving."

"Yep. Sounds good."

"Pizza or tacos?"

"Tacos."

"Great. I know a great place a few miles from here," he told me as he started the truck.

As he pulled out onto the main road, I asked, "When the hell have you been to Sacramento?"

"My sister moved out here a couple of years ago. I come down every so often to check on her and the kids."

"And you take her out for tacos?"

"Hell, no. She takes me," he laughed. "Forewarning, the place doesn't look like much, but they make a mean fucking taco, man."

He wasn't lying when he said it wasn't much. Hell, the place looked like it should've been condemned. "This is the place?"

"The one and only." As soon he parked the truck, he jumped out and started for the door. By the time I'd made it inside, he'd already gotten to the front of the line and was ready to place our order. "You want the special?"

"I'll have what you're having."

"Got it."

I sat down in one of the booths and waited for him to bring our tray of food over. He was smiling like a kid on Christmas as he plopped down in the seat across from me. "Damn, these look even better than last time."

He took one of the huge tacos off his plate and took a bite. A huge smile spread across his face as his chewed. Following suit, I took one of my own and tried it, and I had to admit, they were really fucking good. Neither of us talked as we finished them off. "You did good, man."

"Told you they were awesome."

I shifted in my seat as I reached for my wallet, but I stopped when I got a glimpse of the man leaving the restroom. His cap was pulled down over his eyes, but I knew it was him the second I saw the familiar scar on his cheekbone. Everything stilled -- the incessant chatter, the music playing in the background -- and there was only the sound of my pulse pounding in my ears. Like he didn't have a care in the world, Lenny walked past me and out the front door. Adrenaline rushed through me as I stood up and growled, "Let's go. Now!"

With Ryder following close behind, I charged out of the front door and scanned the parking lot for any sign of him. It had only been a few seconds, if that, but he was gone. "What's wrong, boss?"

"Lenny DeMarco."

Ryder knew all about Lenny and Joey DeMarco. He'd been there when Murray and I had hunted them down and burned through their contacts. He knew we were hungry for revenge and wouldn't stop until we had it. He knew the name was important and saw me frantically looking around, so he asked, "You think you saw him or something?"

"Oh, I saw him. There's no fucking doubt about that. I just can't figure out where the motherfucker went."

"We'll find him. What was he wearing?"

"Dark jeans. Red Polo. Black ball cap."

"Let's get in the truck and see if we can figure out

where he went."

Each minute we spent driving, the farther into the darkness I fell. All the memories of Lainey and my father came crashing over me. Memories of the blood, the smell of gun powder, and the gut wrenching feeling of loss invaded my mind, making it impossible to think of anything except my overwhelming need for revenge. He was close. I could feel it in my bones, and I'd be damned if I was going to let him get away. Hell fucking no. Not this time.

Chapter 16

Tristen

I made good use of my free day. With Max's help, I managed to get all my books for my new classes and even convinced him to run by the grocery store for some decent cereal and something other than ramen noodles. Once we got back, I organized my closet and drawers, putting all of my things back where they belonged. While I kept most of the things he'd bought, there were several things that I decided Josie might like and bagged them up for her. By the time I'd finished, I was exhausted, so I took a hot bath and went to bed. I lay there for several hours, thinking Nathan would finally make it home, but he never did. I woke up the next morning to an empty bed, so I went on to work and hoped he'd be there when I got off. Again, there was no sign of him. I tried to convince myself that nothing was wrong, and he was just busy with work, but it hurt that he hadn't called or even sent a text message. When he hadn't shown up by the third day, it was impossible for me not to be worried, and a little mad. Yes, I was mad. So, I decided to send him a message.

Me:

Are you okay?

Damaged Goods

Nathan:
Everything's fine. Working. Will call later.

I'd like to say that he eventually called, but he didn't. I went to work and met Tony at the bar. As promised, he started my training, and instead of my working my normal tables, I spent the night working alongside him at the bar. The fast pace and talking with the customers gave me a much-needed distraction. I'd been able to push thoughts of Nathan to the back of my mind and focus on work, until I looked up and found Max sitting at the counter. Worried that something was wrong, I rushed over to him.

"Is something wrong?"

"Nope. Everything's fine." He motioned his hand towards one of the TVs behind me. "I just decided to come inside and watch the game instead of listening to it out in the car. Mind getting me a glass of water?"

After I poured him a glass, I set it on the counter in front of him and asked, "Are you sure nothing's wrong?"

"What makes you think something's wrong?"

"Maybe the fact that Nathan's been MIA for the last three days? He hasn't even called me once, or sent a message to let me know that he's alive. Nothing. I'd say that's something to be worried about."

"Really?" he asked, sounding surprised.

"Really. Not even once." His face twisted into a grimace. "Just tell me if I should be worried. Has he changed his mind about me or…?"

"No."

"Then, what is it?"

"He's working."

"Are you sure that's all there is to it?"

"When it comes to his work, it can be complicated."

"Everything with him is complicated." The crowd was really thinning out, so I started wiping down the bar. "I just don't get why it has to be so damn hard!"

Max shrugged his shoulders as he replied, "Nothing worth having is ever easy." He took a drink of his water, then looked back at the TV screen as he said, "Think of it like a game of baseball. You'll always get curve balls. You just have to decide whether to hit the ball or let it fly by."

"I don't know. When it comes to Nathan, I feel like I'm standing there waiting for a ball that might never come."

"You'll never know unless you try."

"Blah. Blah. Enough about Nathan. My mind can't take any more." I threw my rag down on the counter and started stocking the glasses for the following day. "Let's talk about you."

"Let's not."

"Come on," I pleaded. "Tell me something about you that I don't know."

"This is not a good game, Tristen. There's nothing entertaining about me."

"I seriously doubt that. How about your dad? Tell me something about him."

A disgruntled look crossed his face as he sighed. "He was a military man. Hard as nails, and after he was medically discharged, he only got worse."

"Why was he medically discharged?"

"He was in Afghanistan. There was some kind of ambush, and he was shot. He lost some of the mobility in his shoulder, so they discharged him."

"You said he got worse. What does that mean?"

Like he was trying to blow it off, he gave me a quick shrug and a lopsided smile. "Mean is one thing. Mean and drunk is an entirely different thing altogether."

Sensing that the conversation was bringing him down, I tried a different avenue. "So, what about your mother?"

His expression softened as he replied, "Best woman I know."

"Were you two close?"

"You could say that." He smiled as he lifted his glass up to his mouth. After he took a drink, he continued, "I guess you could say she was both a mother and a father. She was always there, no matter what it was... my baseball games, the day I got my first job, my graduation, and even the day I joined the Marines. I could always count on her."

"She sounds like a wonderful mom."

"She was." Max looked around the room and saw

that it was empty. "You about ready?"

"Sure, let me grab my stuff. I went back to the staff room to get my purse and to let Tony know I was leaving, and then I met Max back out front. Once we were in the car, I turned to him and asked, "So, you were in the Marines?"

"I was. For almost three years," he answered as he started the car and headed back towards the condo.

"How did you go from being in the Marines to working for Nathan?"

"I was on leave and flying home. We were on the plane together and got to talking."

"Seriously? You two just started chatting, and you agreed to be his bodyguard?"

"I'm not exactly his bodyguard, Tristen."

"Then, what are you?"

"It's *complicated*."

"In other words, you can't tell me."

"You're learning."

"I'm trying."

When we got back to the condo, Max followed me upstairs and waited for me to open the door. As I stepped inside, I turned to him and asked, "Is he really okay?"

"He is."

"Okay." I was about to shut the door when a thought came to my mind. "Hey, what's the point of driving me to and from work, and watching over me like a hawk, when you're just going to leave me here alone?"

"I'm not going far, and there are always eyes on this condo. You don't have to worry," he assured me.

"What do you mean you aren't going far?"

"I live in one of the condos below Nitro."

I raised my hands in surrender. "Of course, you do. Don't tell me any more. I'm taking a bath and going to bed."

After my bath, I stepped out in the hall and looked down towards Nathan's room. The door was open, but the lights were out, making it seem empty and dark. I just couldn't face sleeping in there alone again, so I crawled into my bed and pulled the covers over me. Feeling a twinge of hope, I reached for my phone and checked the screen. My heart sank when I saw that he still hadn't called or messaged me. With my phone in my hand, I laid back on my pillow and started flipping through my old pictures. There were several of me and the girls at the club and then they rolled into pictures I'd taken with Josie. Just seeing her face made me miss her. I looked at the time and knew it was late, but against my better judgement, I called her.

It had only rung once before she answered, "What's wrong?"

"Nothing's wrong. I was just calling…."

"Tristen, do you have any idea what time it is?"

"I'm sorry. I shouldn't have called so late. I just got home from work and was looking through some of our pictures. I wasn't thinking."

"Are you sure you're okay?" I could hear the worry in her voice, which made me regret calling her even more.

"I'm fine. I guess I was just missing you a little."

"Oh, sweetie. It's okay. I miss you, too. Maybe we could meet for lunch or something one day this week."

"I'd like that."

"Was work okay tonight?"

She was fishing, but I decided to just ignore it. "It was really good, actually. They are training me to run the bar. I've still got a lot to learn, but I'm pretty excited about it. I'll be making much better tips working there."

"That's great."

"And I got my books for my classes. I'll be starting next week."

"That all sounds really good! So, why don't you just tell me what's really bothering you?"

"It's not that big of a deal."

"Okay, then just tell me. It might make you feel better to talk it out."

"Nathan had to go out of town the other day, which isn't a big deal. I know he has his business thing going on."

"But?"

"Well, he hasn't called or checked in since he left. I mean, he responded to my message, but it was short. He basically cut me off."

"So, what exactly are you worried about? Are you thinking he's in some kind of trouble? Or do you think this has something to do with you?"

"That's just it. I don't know."

"Tristen, it's the same way with the guys at the club. You know this. They don't discuss business. As crazy as it sounds, they really do think they're protecting us. They don't realize how crazy it makes us when we don't know what's going on."

"So, you wouldn't be worried if Big hadn't touched base with you in days?"

"No. I didn't say that," she scoffed. "I'm saying it's something that goes with the territory. I knew that going in, so I can't really fuss about it when it happens, and it does happen, Tristen. More than I'd care to admit."

"I guess."

"Has there ever been a time when you didn't talk to him every day?"

"Yes."

"And was everything okay when you finally did see him?"

"Yes."

"Okay. Then, I think you have your answer."

"You're right. I've just been worried."

"Well, stop. At least until you know you have something to worry about."

"Okay. I'll stop freaking out. Thanks for listening."

"That's what I'm here for, and I'm serious. Let's get together for lunch this week. Just text me when you have a free day, and I'll come meet you."

"I'll check my schedule and let you know."

"Sounds good. Now, get some sleep."

"Will do. Night, Josie."

While I felt better after talking to her, the ache was still there, creeping over me in the quiet of the night. I rolled to my side and looked at the empty spot next to me, and even though he wasn't there, I could still feel him, smell him, and I wanted him home. I missed him. Without even realizing I was crying, tears started to stream down my face. It would've been one thing if it were only about his business, but in my heart, I truly believed there was something more going on. The thought of him shutting me out hurt. I hated that it bothered me so much, but there was nothing I could do to stop the dull ache in my heart. Giving in to my own sadness, I let myself cry, praying that the next day things would be different.

Chapter 17
Nitro

"What do you think of the name Lila?" Lainey whispered softly. It was late, but neither of us could sleep. We'd gone to her latest OB appointment and found out we were having a girl. I didn't care if the baby was a boy or a girl as long as it was healthy. I knew I loved her the minute I'd found out she'd been conceived, but I could tell Lainey was relieved. She was worried she wouldn't know what to do with a boy, even though I'd told her I had plenty of experience in that area. For some reason, though, that didn't set her mind at ease. After we'd gotten the results, we'd gone by to see her parents. Once we'd told them the news, we stopped over at Mom and Pop's to tell them. By the time we got home, we were both wiped and crashed on the bed.

"I like Lila, but I thought we were going with the name Grace."

She ran her hand over her round belly and smiled. "We were, and I love the name, but...."

"Are you changing your mind?" I teased.

"Maybe."

I rolled to my side and faced her, placing my hand next to hers on her belly. "I'm sure peapod will love whatever name you choose. For that matter, we could just use both names and call her Lila Grace."

Her eyes lit up as she looked at me. "Lila Grace. That's the perfect name."

"It is."

"I love you, Nathan."

She leaned over and was just about to press her lips to mine when all of the color drained from her face and she frantically moved her hands to the side of her belly. Her eyes dropped to the blood gushing from her bullet wound. Her hands were soaked in blood as she cried, "Nathan! Help me!"

"*Lainey*!" I shouted as I reached for her, but her image started to fade, leaving me grasping at nothing but the pile of pillows at my side. My eyes flew open, and I was wet with sweat as I sat up in the bed. I looked around the dark hotel room and shouted as I threw one of the pillows across the room. "Goddammit!"

I was running on empty—only a few hours of sleep in the last three days and barely a bite to eat. I knew I needed to pull myself together, but that old darkness had found its way back into my heart. I'd tried to fight it, but the need for vengeance had burned through me with no regard for anything else. I was tired, angry, and frustrated to the point that I wanted to yell and scream to let it all out, but like always, I kept it bottled up inside. There was no point in losing it. The DeMarco brothers had a debt to pay, and no matter how long it took, I was going to make sure that they both paid in full.

Damaged Goods

It had been three days since I'd seen Lenny in that fucking taco restaurant, and I'd nearly convinced myself that I'd imagined the whole damn thing until we got our first lead. It had taken some time, but with our contacts in the area, we'd found out that Lenny and Joey were going by different names, Manny and Dash. We'd also discovered that they were working with a guy named Calhoun, a big dog who ran many drug and prostitution rings in several cities, including Seattle—just a few hours from home. We were getting close. I could feel it in my bones. It was only a matter of time before we found them.

I'd managed to get a couple hours of sleep before the dreams set in. I knew that once they started, they wouldn't stop, so I got up and went downstairs to the hotel lobby for a cup of coffee. I sat down with my coffee at a corner table and tried to watch the news. Their voices seemed muffled by the chaos going on in my head, and I could feel my impatience rising. Even though I'd only been sitting there a few minutes, I was becoming restless, so I took my coffee and headed upstairs. I was just about to step on the elevator when I ran into Ryder. "Why haven't you been answering your phone?"

"Why? What's going on?"

"Nothing. I just figured you'd want to hit the ground running this morning."

"I do. I just came down for a cup of coffee."

"I see that. I could use one of those myself," he

grumbled as he stepped off the elevator. "That and a pack of cigarettes."

"I'm headed up for a shower. I'll be back in ten, and we can head out."

He nodded and started towards the lobby. I took my shower and rummaged through my bag for the last of my clean clothes. Once I was dressed and had everything sorted, I went back downstairs. I found Ryder out in the parking lot talking on his cell phone. "Thanks, brother. We're headed that way now."

He turned to me and smiled. "We got the motherfucker."

"You got his location?"

"He's with some chick at one of the hotels downtown."

"Anyone else with them?"

"No idea. Guess we'll find out when we get there."

We both got in the rental, and adrenaline surged through me as we headed to the location Ryder's contact had given him. As Ryder started down the road, I only had one thing on my mind—Lenny DeMarco—and everything else faded into the background. Hell, I was too amped up to even know which way we were going. My pulse was racing, and my mind was bombarded with thoughts of coming face to face with Lenny. I wanted to wrap my hands around the motherfucker's throat and watch the life drain from his body. But that death was too easy, too quick. He deserved a long, miserable death, and I was going to make sure that's exactly what he got, as soon as I found his brother. I had to get them both. It was the only way I'd ever find peace.

My thirst for revenge had driven me to the edge, and as we pulled up to the hotel, I had to fight to keep myself under control. Luckily it wasn't crowded; there were just a few people checking out and loading their cars. As soon as Ryder parked the SUV at the curb beside the front door, we both checked our weapons and went inside. Once we were in the lobby, Ryder motioned me over to him.

"I'll do a walkthrough and see if I can find him." I nodded and waited for him to go into the restaurant. Seconds later he came back to the door and said, "He's here. As far as I can tell, it's just him and the girl."

"I want them both."

"How do you want to play this?"

"We wait. When they start to leave, we make our move."

Ryder got us a table at the door which gave us a clear view of Lenny and his girl. Life hadn't been good to Lenny. He'd grown old with thinning hair and thick wrinkles around his eyes and forehead, and his gut had all but doubled. The old, fat fucker was completely oblivious to the fact that we were there watching him. He sat eating his eggs and bacon like everything was right as rain, having no idea that I was about to turn his entire life upside down, just like he'd done mine. I watched with repulsion as he reached for his girlfriend's hand. She was a young blonde, maybe in her late twenties, and she was wearing jeans with heels and a black low cut tank. From the way she looked at him it was clear that she was crazy about him. I wanted to shake her, to tell her all the horrible things he'd done, but I knew a girl like her wouldn't believe it coming from me. But I knew she'd figure it out soon enough.

"They're about to make their move," Ryder told me as he stared in Lenny's direction.

"Let's see which way they go. It'd be best if we could get them both in the parking lot, but we'll make it work either way."

"We need to play this smart, brother. There's no way to be sure who's watching."

"I don't give a fuck," I growled. "I'm not leaving here without them."

Just as the words left my mouth, Lenny and Blondie got up from their table and started walking towards the door. I took a deep breath as they walked by us and past the hostess's desk. To my relief, they were headed out towards the parking lot. "Let's go."

Ryder and I followed close behind as Lenny led his girl over to a new, bright red Audi TTS. Thankfully, most of the people had already packed up and gone, leaving us alone in the parking lot. Just as Lenny opened the passenger door for her, Ryder stepped up behind him and placed the barrel of his gun against his back. Surprise crossed his face as I stepped in front of him and smiled. "Hello, *Lenny*. It's been awhile."

Damaged Goods

As I reached for his girl's hand and moved her away from him, she started to resist, crying and pulling away from me, until I pressed my gun against her temple. She froze with tears streaming down her face as Lenny shouted, "Get your fucking hands off her!"

"That's not gonna happen."

His back stiffened as he glared at me angrily. "What the fuck do you want?"

"I'm here to collect a debt that's been a long time coming, DeMarco."

Ryder jabbed his gun deeper into Lenny's back, "We're gonna take a little ride, motherfucker. Now move!"

"Look… let's talk about this," Lenny stammered. "I've got money… drugs… women. Anything you want. Surely, we can work something out."

"Like you worked things out with my father, you piece of shit? Now, move your ass, or I'll put a bullet in her pretty little head."

"Manny!" the blonde yelped as I pushed her forward.

"I'll do whatever you want… just let her go!"

"Where's your brother?"

"I don't know," he lied.

With her whimpering and blubbering like an idiot, I pushed the girl forward, forcing her towards the SUV as I said, "That was your one and only chance, Lenny."

After we got them in the truck, Ryder took Lenny's phone, tossed it to the ground, and then zip-tied both their hands and feet. My hands were literally shaking from all the adrenaline as I covered their mouths with duct tape. After all that time, it had finally happened. I'd found him.

Once we had them secured in the backseat, Ryder slammed the door and walked over to me. "What's the plan?"

"We're taking them back to Washington."

"Why not just end the fucker here?"

"This isn't over until I get his brother, too." I got in the passenger seat as I said, "We need to go by the hotel, grab our shit, and get the fuck out of here."

When we pulled out onto the road, I was thankful for the darkly tinted windows. The last thing we needed was for someone to see that we had two people bound and gagged in the backseat. Ryder pulled up to the back of the hotel and waited as I went in to grab our stuff. In less than twenty minutes, we were back on the road and headed to Washington. Lenny's muffled grunts and groans echoed through the truck as he fought against his restraints, and I relished in the sound of him being scared out of his mind. I wanted him scared. I wanted him completely terrified, just like Lainey and my father had been the night he'd killed them. I wanted him to suffer like they had, and by the time I was done with him, he'd be praying for fucking mercy.

We drove straight through, only stopping for gas and necessary breaks, and managed to make it back home before midnight. We took them to one of my warehouses up in the mountains. It was a more discreet location, one where no one would think to look for them. We got them out of the truck and took them inside. Ryder took the girl into a separate room, while I led Lenny into the back of the warehouse. This particular warehouse had once been used as a deer processing center, so there was a large freezer in the back. Panic washed over him as I took him inside and secured him to a chair in the center of the room. As soon as I ripped the tape from his mouth, the incessant pleading began.

"Just let me go. I'll give you whatever you want. Anything. Just name it."

"The one thing I truly want, you can't give me, Lenny. You took that away from me ten years ago."

"It wasn't me. I didn't do anything. I swear. Just let me go."

"You didn't go into my father's house and put a bullet in his head? You didn't shoot my mother and Lainey? You didn't kill my *unborn daughter*?" Rage surged through me as my fist grew taut, and I slammed it across his jaw. Once the first punch was thrown, I couldn't stop. I just kept hitting him, over and over again, while I cursed his very existence.

I was still laying into him when Ryder came up to the door. "Nitro."

Forcing myself to take a step back, I looked down at Lenny hunched over in his chair, seeing his swollen and bleeding face, and I had to fight the urge to pull out my gun and just end him right then and there. I took in a deep breath, and walked over to Ryder, closing the door behind me. "Yeah?"

"It's nearly two in the morning."

"What are you talking about? We just got here."

"You've been back here wailing on him for over two hours, man. There's not going to be anything left of him if you keep going at this rate. You need to go home and catch your breath."

"The fuck I do."

"You do, brother. You haven't slept in days." He took a step towards me with concern in his eyes. "You've been waiting ten long years for this, and now, you're closer than you've ever been."

"I'm not leaving here until I know where his brother is."

"Christ, man. You're never gonna get it out of him if you kill him the first night. You've gotta take a step back. You have my word, we'll get it out of him, but for now, you can't keep going like this. You're going to end up doing something you regret and fucking everything up."

"Fuck you, Ryder. I'm not going anywhere."

"Just hear me out, boss. Go home. Even if it's just for a couple of hours. Get some sleep, and I'll stay here. I'll keep an eye on things until you get back."

"I won't be able to sleep, Ryder. Not knowing he's here."

"You need to try. Besides, it will give you a chance

to talk to Max. We're going to need his help if we want to find Joey... and check on your girl. I know she'll want to see your sorry ass, but take a shower first. You don't want to freak her out with all that blood on your hands and clothes."

I looked down at my hands and shirt, and he was right. I was covered in that motherfucker's blood. With a defeated sigh, I said, "Fine, but I'll be back in a few hours. I'm trusting you to make sure he doesn't go anywhere."

"Look at him, boss. That piece of shit isn't going anywhere, but I won't take my eyes off him. He'll be right here waiting when you get back."

Knowing he was right, I nodded and headed out to the SUV. The drive home was a long one. It was hard to leave there without finishing what I'd started and getting the answers I wanted, but deep down, I knew Ryder was right. At the rate I was going, I was going to fuck things up and kill the motherfucker before we'd found Joey. Whether I liked it or not, I had to be patient. By the time I pulled into the condo's parking garage, it was almost three in the morning. I knew Tristen would be asleep, so I did my best not to wake her as I went inside. When I got to my room, I was surprised to see that she wasn't sleeping in my bed, but I decided it was for the best as I went into the bathroom to take a shower. With the hot water streaming down my back, I thought how good it would feel to have her arms wrapped around me, letting her touch bring me back to humanity, but I was torn. I didn't want her to know the beast inside of me had been released, that he'd taken over my every thought, and he wouldn't let go until the deed was done. I figured it was best I didn't even see her, fearing I might lose her if she saw me in that state, but I was a selfish asshole. I needed her, even if it was just for a brief moment, so without even dressing, I went into her room and got in the bed next to her. I didn't want to talk. I didn't want to explain my reasons for being gone or not calling her. I just wanted to feel her body next to mine and calm the monster inside long enough for me to sleep.

Chapter 18
Tristen

I thought I was only dreaming, that I hadn't really felt the mattress dip as Nathan slipped into bed next to me. I thought the warmth of his body and the rough bristles of his day-old beard against my neck were just figments of my imagination. It wasn't until I felt his hand trail up my thigh that I realized it was really him. My breath caught as his fingers curled around the band of my lacy panties and slid them down over my hips. "Nathan?"

He didn't answer. Instead, his hands reached for my t-shirt and gently pulled it over my head. I wanted to protest and plead with him to talk to me, but it felt so good to have him so close. I'd missed him. I'd missed his touch and his mouth against my skin, and I just couldn't tell him to stop. He eased himself down the bed and placed his head at my center as his tongue brushed roughly against me, causing my back to arch against the mattress. Needing to hear his voice, I tried once again. "Nathan, are you okay?"

Giving no response whatsoever, he continued to torment me with his mouth. There was something different about the way he touched me, though. It wasn't his usual sensual caress. Like a man possessed, his touch was rough and demanding, but it felt so damn good. Every nerve in my body tingled as his warm, wet mouth pressed against me, and just when I thought I couldn't take it anymore, I realized he was just getting started. His fingers delved inside me, twisting and turning as he dragged them across my g-spot. Jolts of pleasure surged through me as he brought me to the edge, making it impossible to resist him. My hands dropped to his head, my fingers tangling in his damp hair as I urged him on, and I prayed that he wouldn't stop. That familiar tingling sensation began to churn in my abdomen, and my body clamped down around his fingers. While I was still dazed by the high of my orgasm, his hands dropped to my hips, and he flipped me over onto my hands and knees.

I turned back to look at him and saw that hungry look in his eyes as he positioned himself at my center. I wanted to say something, to tell him that I'd missed him or that I was glad he was home, but I didn't get that chance. He reached for my hair, pulling firmly and forcing me to look forward as he thrust deep inside me. It was then that I knew it wasn't about making love. That moment had nothing to do with me and him. It was about him—only him. He needed the release, to let go of whatever was weighing on him, and I was simply a means to an end. My feelings were hurt, but my body didn't seem to be fazed by the insult. He felt too damn good, and I was helpless under the spell of his touch. The sounds of our bodies colliding echoed through the room as he drove into me, again and again, each move more demanding than the last. His body tensed as his fingers dug into my hips, and I knew he was getting close. He pulled my hair harder as a growl vibrated through his chest, and his rhythm grew more demanding. While the man behind me wasn't the man I'd grown to love, I knew he was in there, hiding in the darkness. I wanted to find a way to reach him and let him know that I was there for him, but he was too far gone. Nathan's hand left my hair and dropped to my waist as he drove into me one last time, submitting to his release. He remained there for several seconds before he ran his hand down my back and lowered himself onto the bed.

Trying to hide the tears that were threatening to fall, I rushed to the bathroom and closed the door. I leaned my back against the wall as I tried to calm my breathing. A flood of emotions consumed me, each one tugging at me and making me feel even more frustrated. I let the anger rise inside of me, knowing it was the only thing that could protect me from the pain. Over the past few days, he'd pushed me to the side like I meant nothing to him, and it hurt more than I cared to admit. I'd missed him. I needed him to show me that he'd missed me, too, but he wouldn't even talk to me, much less look at me. I'd thought we were getting somewhere, that he was finally letting me in, but suddenly he had me wondering if I'd been wrong about everything. Feeling angry and disappointed, I started to clean myself up, and that's when I realized it was the first time we'd had sex without a condom. My night just kept getting worse, and I wondered if he even cared.

By the time I walked back into the bedroom, Nathan was sound asleep. Once again, he gave no sign that he was concerned about me in the least. I let the anger come as I crawled back into the bed next to him. I needed it to cover my own weakness as I looked at him lying there. Even though I was upset with him, I longed for him. He didn't make it easy, but I loved him. I loved him more than I even realized, and I hated that he was putting his walls back up and shutting me out. I worried that the walls might be too thick or too high, and I wouldn't be able to get past them. The mere thought of losing him ripped at my heart. I ran my fingers through his tousled hair and trailed them along the curve of his jaw and down his arm. When I reached his hands, I finally noticed the deep cuts and scrapes across his knuckles. I sat up in the bed to get a closer look and winced as I saw that they were swollen and bleeding. Worried that they might become infected, I went to the bathroom for the first aid kit. Once I'd found it, I sat down on the floor next to him and started to clean and wrap his wounds. I desperately wanted to know what had happened, but unfortunately, I didn't get the chance to ask.

By the time I woke up the next morning, he was gone. I would've thought I'd dreamed the entire thing if I hadn't spotted his bloody bandages on the nightstand. Seeing them there gave a whole new meaning to the saying, 'love 'em and leave 'em.' It was impossible not to be hurt, but more than that, I was angry. I wanted answers, and I knew there was only one way I was going to get them. So, I took a quick shower, got dressed, and went to find Max. As I walked into the kitchen, my mood hung over me like a big, dark cloud, and with each step it continued to grow darker and larger until it was all consuming. I was hoping that a cup of coffee and a chat with Max might help the clouds pass, but that didn't happen. Instead, my mood only got worse as I discovered that Max had been replaced by a young, burly guy with tattoos and the same tired expression Nathan had had the night before.

"Who are you?"

"Ryder."

"That's all you got?"

"What else do you want?" he snapped back, clearly grumpy as hell. He ran his hands over his face as he shook his head and yawned. "I'm sorry about that. I'm just wiped the hell out. I'm one of Nitro's guys. I'm here to run you to work. You ready to go?"

"Hold on a minute. Where's Max?"

"He's working."

"He's usually here."

"Well, I'm here. He's with Nathan today."

I was becoming frustrated and angrier by the minute. "I take it you aren't going to tell me what the hell is going on? Or why Nathan's been gone? Or why his hands were beat all to hell, and he looked like a damn mess last night?"

"You're right. I'm not."

I didn't like him, not even a little, and his flippant attitude made me want to punch him in the throat. "Will you at least tell me if he's okay?"

"He's fine. Now, are you ready for work or what?"

"I'm ready," I snapped. "I just need to get my purse."

I stormed off to my room and returned to find Ryder waiting with the front door open. "Ready when you are."

I charged past him and on to the elevator, choosing not to speak or acknowledge him in any way. I remained tight lipped until he pulled up at the restaurant. "So, are *you* coming to get me, or should I find my own way back home after work?"

"Someone will be coming for you. If I'm *lucky*, it won't be me."

"That goes for *both* of us." It was at that point, I decided that he was the biggest asshole I'd ever met. I got out of the car and slammed the door. When I got inside, I went straight to the staff room to change. I started to undress, completely oblivious to the fact that Ava was sitting in the corner fixing her makeup.

"Damn, girl. What's with you today?"

Startled, I jumped and yelped, "Shit, you scared the hell out of me."

"I've been standing here the whole time. It was like you were in your own world when you walked in here."

"Sorry. It was a bad morning."

"I can see that. You want to talk about it?"

"Men are assholes. All of them."

"Amen, sister. Are you just figuring that out?" she laughed.

"I guess I've always known it. I've just been waiting for one of them to prove me wrong."

"No such luck?"

"Not yet."

"Well, don't give up. I have a feeling if one's to be found, you'll find him."

"Ha!" I scoffed as I finished buttoning my shirt. "I wouldn't hold my breath."

"So, what happened? Was it regular stupid guy stuff, or was it something more?"

"I'd have to say this is more than the regular stupid guy stuff, but I'll get over it. I'm sure it's just a misunderstanding."

"Okay. If you say so." She stood up and placed her makeup bag away. "But I'm here if you want to talk about it."

"Thanks, girl." As we started toward the front, I remembered seeing her leave with some guy I'd never seen before. "Hey, I forgot to ask. Who was that hot guy I saw you leaving with the other night?"

"That was Lucas." Her voice fell flat as she said his name. "We've been off and on for months. I think it's time to face the fact that it just isn't going to work out."

"Any particular reason why?"

"He has an issue with keeping his dick in his pants." She frowned as she shrugged her shoulders. "There was a time when I thought I'd found the one. I guess that's why it's so hard to let him go."

Just before I turned to go to the bar, I looked back at her. "If he doesn't get how great you are, then you're better off without him."

As she started walking away, she smiled and replied, "Maybe you should take some of your own advice."

"Girl, you're probably right."

As I slipped behind the counter, I hoped that my day might get a little better. Unfortunately, that didn't happen. My mind was on Nathan, which meant I was distracted, which meant I kept screwing up my orders. I couldn't help myself. Like slow waves, thoughts of him crept over me, bringing another round of heartache. Tony tried to be patient, but I could tell he was getting frustrated with me. I tried to pull it together, and thankfully, after a half-hour or so, I started to get back on track. I was just getting into the swing of things when the lunch rush ended and things started to slow down. I was about to do a round of refills when I spotted Josie sitting at the end of the counter.

"Hey!" I smiled as I walked over to her. "I didn't know you were coming by."

"I tried to call, but I guess you were busy."

"Sorry, it's been a little crazy here today."

"Do you get a break anytime soon?"

"I can take one in a few minutes. Can you wait a sec while I cash out?"

"Sure." She smiled. "I have an hour before I have to leave for class."

As soon as I finished up with my last two customers, I went over to Tony and told him I was going to take my break a little early. After he gave me the okay, I grabbed two bottles of water and led Josie out onto the restaurant's back patio. Once we sat down, I asked her, "Is everything okay?"

"I was just about to ask you the same thing. I've been worried since our talk the other night."

"I'm sorry I worried you, but I'm fine. Nathan's home, and everything's better already," I lied.

"Are you sure?"

I nodded as I took a drink of my water. "Yes, Josie. I'm sure. Now, stop worrying."

"Okay. Okay. I'll leave it, but if you need anything… I'm here."

"I know. That's why I called you in the first place," I teased. "Oh, I forgot to tell you. I have some clothes to give you."

"What clothes?"

I wasn't sure how to explain the whole debacle over the clothes Nathan had bought, so I decided to skip it altogether. "I hit a great sale the other day and found a few things I thought you'd like."

"That was so sweet. I can't remember the last time I've been shopping."

"There are a couple of things I thought you could wear to the club or out riding with Big."

"Awesome. Thanks for doing that."

"I'll bring them over the next time I come by."

"That sounds great." She stood up as she said, "I guess I better get going. I need to get gas before I go to class."

"I'm glad you stopped by." I gave her a quick hug. "But I still want us to do lunch soon."

"Just let me know when and where, and I'll be there."

"You got it." I followed her back into the restaurant and just as she started for the front door, I called, "Tell Big I said hi!"

"I will! Have a good one!"

I headed back to the bar and tried to get things in order before the dinner crowd started rolling in. As I stocked the glasses, I thought about my visit with Josie, and I wasn't sure why I hadn't just told her about Nathan. It would've helped to hear her take on things, but I was afraid I might hear something I didn't like. I knew things weren't going the way I'd hoped between us, but I loved him, and I wasn't ready to give up on him yet.

Chapter 19
Nitro

The sun was just starting to rise when I pulled myself out of Tristen's bed. I looked down at her, sleeping so peacefully, and I wanted to believe that my actions hadn't hurt her last night. I should've stayed away, but I just couldn't resist the temptation. I needed a second to forget, to feel her next to me and let go of the anger, but she deserved more than that. Even after I'd handled things wrong, she'd only shown me compassion and understanding, even when I didn't deserve it. She'd shown me a glimpse of the light, given me a hunger for it, and I knew dealing with my past was the only way to completely erase the darkness. As much as I hated leaving her without setting things straight, I knew it wouldn't be possible until I ended things with Lenny and Joey. So, I removed the bandages Tristen had put on my wounds and got dressed. After I found Max and explained everything to him, he started the hunt for Joey. I knew that even though Max was good, it would take time to find him, time I didn't have. It wouldn't be long before word got out that Lenny was missing, and fearing for his own life, Joey would go deeper into hiding.

As soon as I made it to the warehouse, I sent Ryder over to the condo to tend to Tristen. After he'd gotten her to work, I knew he'd need to get some sleep, so it was up to Max and me to finish this thing. While Max was putting out feelers looking for Joey, I went to have a chat with Lenny. With my black duffle bag, I walked into the room, and I was surprised to see how fucked up he looked. His eyelids were nearly swollen shut, bruises covered his face and body, and his hair was matted with sweat and blood. He was barely able to keep his head up as I walked into the room and lowered my bag to the floor. Ryder had been right to make me leave. One more good hit, and the motherfucker wouldn't have been breathing.

Lenny's attention was drawn to the bag at my feet as I sat down in the chair in front of him and crossed my arms. "Morning, Lenny. How ya feeling?"

"Fuck you."

"That good, huh?"

"Why don't you just kill me and get it over with?" he grumbled.

"I could do that, but you're going to have to do some talking first."

"I have nothing to say to you." I leaned over and unzipped my bag. With his voice raised in panic, he shouted, "What are you doing?"

I pulled out a billy club and rested it in my lap. "Where is your brother, Lenny?"

"I already told you I don't know."

"I hate to hear that Lenny." I stood up with the billy club in my hand and started for the door.

"Where are you going?" he shouted as I walked out

of the room.

His girl was next door, and as much as I hated to do it, I was going to pay her a little visit. Her dark brown eyes widened with terror as she watched me walk into the room. When her eyes dropped down to the long, thin billy club, she frantically tried to pull her hands out of her restraints, but it was useless. I walked over to her and with one quick yank, I ripped the tape from her mouth. As I'd hoped, she let out a high-pitched scream. I tossed a rope over one of the rafters and then grabbed her hands, pulling her to her feet. "*Please...* Please don't. I'm begging you."

Ignoring her, I used the rope to tie her hands over her head, forcing her to remain standing. I stood in front of her, just inches from her face and asked, "Where's Joey?'

"I don't even know anyone named Joey. I swear. I have no idea who you're talking about."

"Lenny's brother.... Where is he?"

"I don't know Lenny, either!"

"The fuck you don't." Fighting the urge to wrap my hands around her throat, I growled, "Manny! Where is Manny's fucking brother?"

"Oh, you mean Dash?"

"Yes, sweetheart. That's exactly what I mean."

"I haven't seen him in weeks. I don't know. Honestly, I don't."

"Where was the last place you saw him?"

"He came down to see Manny about work, and then

we went to eat dinner after. That was it," her voice trembled.

"Have you ever gone to see him?"

"A couple of times, I guess."

"Where?"

"It was a different place each time. Some restaurant in Seattle is all I know. I promise."

Something in her voice let me know she was telling the truth, which meant Lenny was my only hope of finding him. I looked at the blonde and asked, "What's your name?"

"Darla."

"Okay, *Darla*. Your boyfriend…"

"Manny is my fiancé. We're supposed to get married next month."

Damn, she was stupider than I thought. "I hate to be the one to tell ya, but that shit ain't gonna happen."

Hoping she was as dramatic as she was stupid, I reached for the billy club. She gasped as I brought it up to her face, then screamed at the top of her lungs, "Manny!"

As I'd hoped, her voice echoed through the warehouse, and I had no doubt he'd heard her screaming. Knowing I had to make him believe I was truly hurting her, I raised the wand and flicked it against her side. As I'd hoped, she immediately started to bellow and cry like I'd hit her at full force. "Oh, god. Please stop. Manny! Help me!"

I struck her two more times along the backside and

thigh, trying my best not to hit her hard enough to leave a bad bruise. Her screams rattled my ears as she thrashed around acting like I was killing her, and anyone in a five-mile radius would've believed her. My intention had been just to get a few yelps out of her, but her little show was better than I could've asked for. Her face was red and full of tears as I told her, "You did good, sweetheart. Now, I'm going back to talk to Lenny, and if you're lucky, I won't have to come back in here."

"No… wait," she gasped. "Please don't hurt him. He's a good man."

I turned to her with disgust. "You don't really believe that, do you? He's a murderer, and a fucking pimp. There's nothing good about him."

"You're wrong. He'd never hurt anyone."

I walked over to her, firmly grabbing her jaw, and forced her to look me in the eye. "He killed my father. Put a bullet in his head over some fucking deal he fucked up on. Then he shot my mother, but that wasn't enough. No. He kept going. He killed my girl. She was eight months pregnant, and he put a bullet in her stomach killing her and our daughter. He *killed my daughter*!"

"No! I don't believe you. Manny would never do something like that."

"It's time for you to wise up, Darla. The fairy tale is over."

I released my grip on her and gave her one last flick

across the hip with the billy club. Her cries roared through the metal walls as I walked back over to Lenny. I could still hear them as I sat back down on the chair in front of him. I pretended to wipe sweat from my brow as I looked over at him and grimaced. "You've got yourself a real fighter over there."

"She's just one of the prostitutes from the club. I don't give a fuck what you do to her," he tried to convince me. "She means nothing to me."

"Is that right?"

"You're just wasting your time with her."

"I don't know about that. I was rather enjoying beating the hell out of her. I might just have to go back for more," I told him as I stood up. "I found it very therapeutic."

As I started walking back towards the door, he shouted, "Please! Just leave her the fuck alone. She has nothing to do with any of this."

"I'll ask you again. Where's Joey?"

"It was all me. Joey had nothing to do with the shooting."

"So, you're telling me he wasn't there that night? He didn't shoot my mother?"

"No! It was me. All *me*," he lied.

I walked back over to the chair and sat down. "Why don't we take a step back? Tell me why you did it."

"Your father was a stubborn, old man. He wouldn't listen. We just needed a few extra days, but he wasn't having it."

"He'd already given you one extension. What made you think he'd ever give you another?"

"We weren't asking for long. Just a few days. Back then, we were just starting out. He knew how hard it was to get a business like ours going, but he didn't give a fuck about that. He left us no choice."

"How did you know where he lived?"

"I had one of my guys follow him home. When we got there, I was expecting to have a harder time getting in, but we walked right in."

His swollen eyes widened when he realized what he'd just said, but it was too late. It was already out there. I knew then, he wasn't alone. "And then?"

My pulse raced with fury as he continued. "They were in the living room. I was just there for your father. I honestly had no intention of hurting anyone else, but it all happened so fast. I had no choice. It was too risky to leave them alive."

"He was dead. The threat was over, so why'd you leave town?"

"We were just planning to lay low for a little while. Let the muddy water clear, but then we got word that you were looking for us, and you'd killed off Drake and Mansfield. We knew you were out for blood, and with Drake gone, we didn't have a choice but to leave town and start over."

It was getting late, and I was tired of talking. I didn't want to hear any more of his bullshit. "Where's Joey, Lenny?"

"It doesn't matter, don't you know that?"

"You're not leaving this room until I find Joey."

"I'm not leaving this room either way, so why should I tell you a damn thing?"

"There's two ways a man can die, Lenny. Short and painless, or long and filled with agony. It's your choice how you go."

"If you want Joey so bad, just wait. He'll be here soon enough." His wicked grin curled across his face. "They'll all be here soon enough."

"What the fuck are you talking about?"

"Did you honestly think I didn't have eyes on me at that hotel? Calhoun watches every fucking move. Nothing gets past him. There have been eyes on you since you pulled out of that parking lot, and they will come for me. But first, they will find your weakness. And you have a weakness, Nitro. Every man has one."

"You're blowing smoke, Lenny," I smiled. "It's a good try, but I'm not buying it."

"Good. I hope you don't."

Max came up to the door and cleared his throat. "Nitro… I found him."

As I stood up, I closed my hand into a fist and slammed into Lenny's face. "Like I told you, motherfucker, one way or another, I'd find him."

I walked out of the room and closed the door. "Where is he?"

"He's been working under Calhoun in Seattle."

"Already knew that."

"I've got the location, but there's no sign of him. My contact thinks he left town."

There was no way of knowing if what Lenny had said was true, so I ordered Max, "It's time to call everyone in. There's a chance we might have trouble coming our way."

"What kind of trouble?"

"Calhoun and Joey. They might've seen us take Lenny from the hotel."

"Any chance someone followed you here?"

"No way. We would've seen them."

"His phone?"

"Ryder got rid of it."

"And hers?"

I shook my head. "I don't remember. It all happened so fast."

"We need to find out. Did she have a purse or anything on her?"

"No purse. Nothing."

"Then, if she had one, it may still be on her."

"Fuck." I turned and headed to the room where we were keeping her.

As soon as I walked in, she started shaking her head and pleading, "No! Please! Not again."

"Where's your phone?"

"What?"

"Your fucking cell phone. Where is it?"

"It's in the front side pocket of my jeans."

When I looked at her jeans, there was no mistaking

the rectangular shape of her phone, and I cursed myself for not seeing it earlier. "Dammit!"

I shoved my hand in her pocket and when I pulled it out, Max said, "Destroy it."

I removed the battery, then slammed it on the ground, shattering into a million pieces. "Make the call."

"It's almost closing time at the restaurant. You want me to go get Tristen."

I looked down at my watch and it was the first time I'd realized how late it really was. "There's no time. Tell Tony to take her, and you meet them there."

"Once I have her, where do you want me to take her?"

I'd fucked up, and it was all coming down on me in a major way. I should've known better, but I was too caught up in getting Lenny's sorry ass. I wasn't thinking of the blowback, and it was going to cost me if I didn't pull my head out of my ass and get this thing done. "Head over to Mom's. Pick her up and take them both over to the safe house."

"You got it." He took a step forward. "We've got this, brother. Let them come. It will only make the job easier."

With that, he turned to leave. Once he was gone, Darla sniffled as she said, "Did he really do all the things you said he did?"

"He did."

"I'm really sorry about your daughter. I had no idea

he could do something like that." She looked down at the floor as she continued, "You should know something... Manny was in some trouble with Calhoun. I figured you were working with him when you came and got us."

"What kind of trouble?"

"I don't know all the details, but I overheard them talking. It had something to do with money, and Calhoun was ready to cut ties with him. I doubt he'd bother to look for him, and he certainly wouldn't send his goons to look for him."

"And Joey?

"If Joey got wind of it, he might come, but there's no way to be sure. One minute they're good, talking all the time and acting like real brothers, and then they're fighting, and all communication just stops."

When I took her, I had all intentions of killing her, but if she was telling the truth, then she'd just helped me in a major way. I reached for her hands, freeing her from the rope, and led her back over to her chair. I watched as her body sank into the seat from exhaustion. "Thanks, Darla. You did good."

"Are you going to let me go?"

Without giving her an answer, I walked out of the room and closed the door. I wanted to believe that she was right about Calhoun, but I wasn't going to take any chances. If he came, I'd be ready. One way or another, I was going to end the DeMarco brothers, and I didn't give a fuck who tried to stand in my way.

Chapter 20

Tristen

The closer we got to closing, the more anxious I became. I had my reasons for being nervous—I'd made up my mind that I was going to try to talk to Nathan. Knowing he had a bad habit of keeping things to himself, I knew it wouldn't be easy to get him to actually open up to me. But if I didn't try, there was a chance he'd just become more distant and even harder to reach. I had to find a way to prove to him that he could trust me, that I would be there for him just like he'd been there for me. I had to try, but I had my doubts he'd listen.

Thankfully, we started shutting down early, so I went to change and get my things. Feeling a little hopeful, I reached for my phone and checked to see if Nathan had messaged me, but yet again, there was nothing from him. There was only a message from Max telling me to catch a ride with Tony to the condo, and that he'd meet us there. Feeling more than a little disappointed, I put my phone in my purse and went up front.

As I walked back out, Tony was waiting for me. "You ready?"

"I'm all set, and hey… I'm sorry about this."

"About what?"

Damaged Goods

"I know it's late. I'm sure you're ready to get home."

"I don't mind. Besides, it's on my way."

I followed him to the back door and waited while he locked everything up. It was dark in the parking lot, but it didn't seem to bother Tony as we walked over to his car. Once we got inside, he smiled and said, "Buckle up, Buttercup."

It amazed me how he was always in a such good mood, even after a long, exhausting day. I rolled my eyes and smiled as I fastened my seatbelt, then looked out the window as he pulled out of the lot. Most of the shops and restaurants around us closed at ten on weekdays, so everything looked deserted as we drove out onto the main road. Tony turned on the radio, and the low hum of an old country song filled the car as we drove. I leaned my head back and closed my eyes as I let the words distract me from the fact that I was heading home. I'd spent the day firing myself up for a big talk, but as we got closer to the condo, I could feel my confidence faltering.

Tony pulled into the garage and parked. "I'll walk you up."

"You don't have to do that," I assured him. "The door is just around the corner."

"Max said he was on his way. Maybe we should wait until he gets here."

I reached for the door handle and said, "Seriously. I can walk a few feet without someone hovering over

221

me."

Just as I started to open my door, I heard the sound of tires screeching. I looked behind the car and saw a white van with black tinted windows parked behind him. "Shut the door!"

I quickly slammed it shut and panic washed over me as I looked over to Tony. "What's wrong? Who is that?"

He grabbed his cellphone and as soon as someone answered, he shouted, "We've got trouble. Get your ass here now!"

He put the car in reverse and tried to back out, but there wasn't enough room. Knowing he was stuck, he pulled a gun out of his glovebox. "I need you to listen to me, Tristen. These guys…."

Before he had a chance to finish his sentence, his window shattered and glass went flying through the car. Tony's head rolled to the side as he faced me. As blood gushed from a bullet hole in his chest, he looked at me with alarm and yelled, "Run!"

I reached for my door handle and was about to try to get out, when I saw a man standing there with a gun pointed directly at me. I froze. Every muscle in my body tightened with fear as I looked frantically around the car. There was no way out, and I'd never felt so terrified. The man pointed his gun towards the door handle, signaling me to unlock it, but I couldn't move. Then, he tapped the barrel against the window, causing me to jump in my seat. "Open the fucking door."

Damaged Goods

I forced my hand to move towards the handle and released the lock. The door flung open, and he reached inside to grab me. His fat fingers pressed into the skin of my forearm and his nails bit into my flesh. As I tried to pull away, tiny beads of blood trickled down my arm.

"Let me go!" I cried as he yanked me from my seat.

"Move your ass." Just as he started to pull me forward, Max's car whipped into the garage and slammed full force into the side of the van. The deafening sound of the crash caused both the man and me to stumble backward with surprise. As soon as Max opened his door, gunfire exploded around us.

When one of the guys dropped to the ground, the driver turned to the man next to me and shouted, "Get her in the goddamn van."

He pulled at my arm, forcing me forward, and I finally got a good look at Max. His gun was drawn and pointed directly at the driver as he continued to move in my direction. I quickly realized it was not the same Max who had greeted me every morning in the kitchen. The calm, sweet Max had been replaced with a man who was hard and a force to be reckoned with. His moves were slow and calculated, making him look menacing as he advanced forward. Without warning, a shot was fired from inside the van causing my heart to drop as I saw that the bullet had hit Max in the shoulder. Seeming unfazed, he pointed his gun towards the van and shot several rounds.

With Max's attention focused on the van, the driver

lunged at him. The garage filled with the sounds of their fists colliding against their bodies, their grunts after each blow, and the shuffle of their feet. Max was holding his own, until the driver jabbed him hard in the ribs and tackled him to the ground. Knowing Max was distracted, the man next to me tightened his grip on my arm and started pulling me towards the back of the van. I tried to fight him, but he was too strong. Like a rag doll, he dragged me. I wasn't a daring person who knew what to do in the heat of the moment. I had to think things through and calculate my next move, but there wasn't time for that. It was all moving too fast, like a blur flashing before my eyes, and I couldn't even form a complete thought.

The man had just opened the van door, when the muffled sound of a gunshot brought everything to a stop. Everything stilled as my heart began to race. I had no idea who had been hit, and the fear that Max had been hurt made my entire body tremble uncontrollably. Time seemed to move in slow motion as I stood there waiting for some sign that he was okay. I looked through the back window and relief washed over me as I spotted Max walking in my direction. He hadn't been shot again, but it was clear that he was hurting. I could see it in the way he moved, but the determined look in his eyes was still there. Apparently the big brute next to me also saw Max, so he began to struggle even more adamantly to get me inside the van. He was trying to push me inside when Max slipped up behind him and snapped his neck. There was no sound, no sign of attack—just a surprised expression on the man's face as his lifeless body fell at my feet.

"We need to move! Now!" Max reached for my hand and led me towards the car. He'd only taken a few steps when another gun shot was fired, this time hitting Max in his side. He tried to hold on to my hand, but the force of the blow was too much, and his body fell to the ground with a hard thud. I'd thought they were all gone, that Max had taken care of all of them, so I had no idea where the shot had come from.

"No, no, no! Max!" Crying, I knelt beside him and placed my hand on his wound, frantically trying to stop the bleeding. His face was twisted in a pained grimace as I pleaded, "Max. I need you to hang on… I need you to be okay. Please, Max."

"Tristen, you have… to get out… of here," he gasped. His eyes widened as a shadow fell over him.

I was too hysterical about Max to notice that the man from inside the van had stepped out and was standing behind me. He reached for my hair and took a fistful in his hand, pulling hard as he jerked me to my feet. "Bitch, get your ass in the goddamn van!"

With my arms flailing, I stumbled back and slammed into the man's chest. I wanted desperately to stay there with Max, but the man gave me no choice as he continued to wrench my hair with one hand and press the gun to my head with the other. "Now!"

With the barrel of his gun at my temple, there was

no way I could fight him, so I did as I was told. I started towards the door and was about to crawl inside when I heard the man say, "Well, look who we have here. It's the man of the hour."

I quickly turned and saw Nathan standing at the front of the van. He pointed his gun in our direction as he snarled, "It's been awhile, Joey."

"Not long enough, if you ask me." The man kept his gun aimed at the side of my head as he snarled, "You know, Lenny kept trying to tell me that we didn't have to worry about you anymore. He said it'd been ten years, and you'd let it go. I knew he was wrong. I knew you would never stop looking for us. As soon as I checked the GPS on Darla's phone and saw that they were headed to Washington, I knew it was you."

"You're right. I won't let it go until you and your brother are six feet under," Nathan growled. He motioned his head towards me as he asked, "So, tell me, Joey... what's your play here?"

"I needed a bargaining chip, and she's it."

"How'd you even know about her?"

"We were already in the county when you and your guy showed up with Lenny and Darla. We followed the GPS out to your warehouse, and we waited there until you left and followed you home."

"Why go to the trouble? You were at the warehouse. You could've come after Lenny then."

"That's just it. I don't give a fuck what happens to Lenny," he snickered. "We had a deal go south a couple of weeks ago, and with him out of the picture, I can make Calhoun think he was the only one behind it."

"And that way, Calhoun will stay off your back."

"Damn straight. I've got a good thing with him. I'm not letting Lenny fuck it up."

I was trying to keep up with the conversation, but it was hard to focus with the barrel of his gun digging into my temple. I looked over to Max, and my eyes widened as I noticed that he had his weapon pointed towards Joey. He motioned his hand to the side, signaling me to try to make a move. I still had no idea why the man wanted to take me, but I knew nothing good could come from me getting inside the van. Knowing I had no choice, I aimed my knee for his midsection and nailed him right between the legs. His breath whooshed from his lungs as he stumbled backward. That's all it took. One moment, one shot, and it was over. The man released his hold on me as his body collapsed towards the van and toppled inside.

When I looked back over to Max, blood was pooling around him and his eyes were closed. "Max!"

As I knelt down beside him, I could see that he was struggling to breathe. "Nathan. We've got to do something."

Nathan lowered himself down next to me as he said, "Max. We're right here. I'm calling for help."

As he took out his phone, he looked over to me and said, "Go over to Tony's car and see if you can find a towel or something we can use to help stop the bleeding."

"Okay."

I rushed over to the car and opened the door. I was searching the backseat when I heard Tony mumble, "You... have to.... get out of... here."

Shocked that he was still alive, I placed my hand on his shoulder and assured him, "It's okay, Tony. Everything is okay. We're calling for help. Just hang on."

I turned to Nathan and shouted, "Tony is still alive, but he's hurt really bad!"

"Find something and place it on the wound. Apply as much pressure as you can, then get back over here." When I looked around the backseat, I found Tony's gym bag sitting in the floorboard. I quickly opened it and found several t-shirts. I took one and placed it on his wound, then reached for his hand and rested it on top of the t-shirt. "Tony, I need you to hold this right here. Don't move it."

I grabbed another shirt and raced over to Nathan and Max. He took the shirt and rolled it into a ball, then pressed it against Max's side. My heart ached as I listened to Nathan talking to him. "Hang in there, brother. I need you to stay with me. You hear me? I need you to fight, Max."

When Max didn't respond, I started to panic. I'd been terrified when those men tried to take me, but that fear was nothing like the fear I felt when I looked at Max. His color was fading, and his breaths were becoming low and shallow. We were losing him. It seemed like we'd been sitting there for an eternity before the ambulance finally arrived. Once they checked his stats, they decided to have him airlifted to the hospital.

While I was a crying, blubbering mess, Nathan remained calm and steady. He helped them load Max onto the helicopter, while the other medics got Tony into the ambulance. Just as they were leaving, the police pulled up and all their attention was directed towards me. They had questions, but I had no idea how to answer them. I still didn't know why those men had come after me, so for the third time, I answered, "I don't know."

"And you don't know why they were trying to take you?" the detective asked.

"No… maybe they thought I was someone else, or maybe they were just looking for a way to get their rocks off. I just don't know."

"You didn't recognize any of them?"

"I've told you. I'd never seen any of them before." I glanced around the garage searching for Nathan. I spotted him staring at me as he talked to one of the policemen. Just knowing he was there helped calm me.

"Do you have any enemies? Someone who might have a grudge against you?" he pushed.

"Not that I can think of. Look, I've already told you everything I know."

"What about the two that just left here with the

medics? Do you know them?"

"Tony is my boss. He was the man in the car. He was just dropping me off from work. The other guy was Max. He works security here at the condo." I knew there was more behind Max's story, but I kept that part to myself. One of the things I'd learned from club was to keep things simple when it came to the police. Besides, with Nathan's line of work, the last thing he needed was a police investigation. "Now, if you don't mind, I need to get to the hospital."

"I understand. We'll contact you if we have any further questions." He reached in his front pocket and pulled out a business card. "If you think of anything we might need to know, just give me a call."

"I will. Thank you," I replied as I started walking towards Nathan. As soon as I reached him, he pulled me closer to him, wrapping his arms tightly around me. His embrace was warm, and his strong arms made me feel protected as he held me close to his chest. My body relaxed against him and the chaos around me melted away as I squeezed him back. He didn't speak. He didn't have to. I could tell how distraught he was by the way he held on to me for dear life.

Chapter 21
Nitro

There are times when a man has to look at the choices he made and decide if they were the right ones. When I finally got my hands on Lenny, everything else fell by the wayside. I hadn't thought about the blowback, or the possibility that someone else I cared about might get hurt, and it'd almost cost me everything all over again. I knew I'd fucked up. I'd gotten caught up in the moment and didn't think things through. I should've taken a step back and calculated a plan, but I was too eager and too desperate to move on with my life. I just prayed that it wasn't too late, and I'd have time to make things right. Despite the heaviness in my chest, I felt a sense of relief at having Tristen back in my arms, feeling her body pressed against mine. Just being close to her soothed me. She was able to take my pain and make it bearable. When Tony had called, I knew it was bad. I could hear it in his voice. I'd tried calling him, over and over again, but I'd gotten no answer. I'd been left in the dark as I raced over to the garage, and I couldn't help but imagine the worst. With it all over and her finally in my arms, the raging beast was forced back into the darkness.

All too soon, she pulled back from our embrace and looked up at me. "We need to get to the hospital."

"We'll run over to county first and check on Tony. We'll see if they can tell us where they decided to take Max." I knew he was going to need major surgery, and county wasn't equipped to handle someone in his condition. "It's going to take them some time to get him stabilized and ready for surgery."

"Okay." She followed me over to the car and got inside. As soon as we hit the main road, the questions started. "Who was that man?"

"Joey was one of the men who killed Lainey and my father."

Her eyes widened for a moment as the words sunk in. "And Lenny is his brother."

"Yes."

"Where is he?"

"At one of my warehouses."

"Is he still alive?"

"He is... for *now*."

Seeming unfazed by the fact that I was going to kill Lenny, she asked, "Is he the reason why you were gone for so long?"

"Yes."

"And why you didn't call or message me for days?"

"Yes."

I could feel the tension rolling off her as she turned and looked out the window. The questions stopped and she became quiet, too quiet. I figured that meant she was overthinking things, or she was pissed and about to blow. Hell, I couldn't blame her. Everything that had happened was my fault. She, Tony, and Max had been caught in the crossfire, and there was nothing I could say to defend myself. Tristen was still looking out the damn window when we pulled up at the hospital. Without looking at me, she got out of the car and started walking inside. Yep, she was pissed.

She walked up to the front desk and said, "I'm here to see Tony Marino."

"Are you family?"

Without skipping a beat, she answered, "I'm his fiancée."

"Come on back," the nurse told her as she opened the door. When I started following, the nurse pointed to the side door. "The waiting room is right around the corner."

Remaining quiet, Tristen kept walking forward without looking back in my direction. Left with no choice, I went to the waiting room and sat down. It was almost fifteen minutes later before Tristen returned. She stopped in the doorway and said, "Max is at Regional. They're prepping him for surgery now."

As soon as I stood up, she turned and started walking towards the front door. She continued outside and over to my car. As soon as she got inside, she buckled her seatbelt and stared out the window. It was a thirty-minute drive to Regional, and the silent treatment had started to get to me, so I asked, "Do you have something you want to say?"

"No."

"I think you do."

"Well, you're wrong."

"I'm sorry you got pulled into this. It wasn't my intention."

"*Seriously*, I don't want to talk about it right now. Max is in the hospital fighting for his life. He's the only thing either of us should be concerned about right now."

"Max is going to be fine."

"How can you be so sure?"

"He's gotten through worse than this before. He'll do it again."

"Who's to say this time he won't? He lost a lot of blood, and he wasn't conscious when they put him in the helicopter. How do you know he has the strength to pull through it this time?" Tears started to trickle down her cheek as she turned away from me. "He put his life on the line for me, and I don't know what I'll do if he doesn't make it."

There was some truth behind her words, and deep down, I knew she was right. Suddenly, I found myself feeling even more anxious to get to the hospital. Without realizing it, I pressed my foot against the accelerator, increasing our speed as we raced down the interstate. When we finally made it, we both rushed inside and went straight to the front desk.

An elderly lady was seated at the help desk and smiled as we approached her. "Can I help you?"

"We're here to see about Max Fisher. Can you tell me where we need to go?"

"Are you a relative?"

Before I answered, Tristen gave me a quick jab in the side with her elbow. "I'm his brother."

Something about saying the words aloud hit me. In every way that mattered, Max was a brother to me. There was never a time that he wasn't there when I needed him, and not just at work. He was there pushing me to be better, encouraging me to do what was right, and he never accepted less than my best. He was there for me in ways that my own brother had never been. I owed him my life, and there wasn't anything I wouldn't do for him. He had to make it. He just had to.

She took a minute to search his name in the computer, and then looked up at me with concern. "Mr. Fisher is in surgery. It's going to be a little while before we know anything. You can sit in the waiting room, and I will have someone come speak to you when they are done."

"I'd appreciate that. Thank you."

I reached for Tristen's hand and led her over to the waiting room. Since it was nearly three in the morning, the place was relatively empty. We walked over to the corner by the TV, and Tristen clung to my hand as we sat down. Like me, she was nervous, but she was trying to keep it together. I looked up at the TV, but I couldn't focus on what they were saying. My head was bombarded with thoughts, making it impossible to think straight. We hadn't been sitting there long when my phone chimed with a text message. I pulled it out of my pocket, and as I looked down at the screen, I saw that it was from Ryder.

Ryder:
Any news on Max?

Me:
He's in surgery now.

Ryder:
Need me to do anything?

Me:
Check in on Tony.

Ryder:
I'm here now. He's in recovery and doing fine.

Me:
Good. Go see about our guests. I'll meet you there when I can.

Ryder:
Will do.

As I placed my phone back in my pocket, I looked down at my lap and saw that Tristen was still holding on to my hand. I wanted to think it was a good sign, but I wasn't so sure. Over the past few weeks, I'd fucked up in more ways than I could count, and I couldn't blame her for having her doubts. Hell, I had plenty of my own. I honestly didn't know if I was capable of giving her the kind of love that she needed. Years ago, I'd given my heart to Lainey and losing her broke me. It had damaged me in ways I couldn't comprehend, and until Tristen, I was fine. I wasn't good, but I was fine. I had my shit together, but Tristen made me want to be better than fine. I wanted to be better for her. I wanted to give her my best. I didn't want to be just fine anymore.

We sat there quietly lost in our own thoughts for over an hour, and Tristen was just about to doze off when a nurse approached us. "Are you here for Max Fisher?"

"Yes. I'm his brother."

"Well, he's out of surgery, and he's stabilized. He'll be in the ICU for the next few hours. If all goes well, they'll put him in his own room."

"So, he's going to be okay?"

"The next few hours are critical. He lost a lot of blood, and the doctor is having a hard time regulating his blood pressure. He just got another blood transfusion, and they are hoping that will help."

"When can we see him?"

"He really needs his rest, but I can take one of you back for a few minutes."

Tristen turned to me and said, "You go. I'm sure he'd like to see you."

I nodded and followed the nurse down the corridor.

My chest tightened as we headed down the second hallway. I hated hospitals. I'd been in them more times than I could count, and just knowing the rooms were filled with people fighting for their lives gave me an uneasy feeling. I knew Max was bad off, but I didn't know just how bad, until I followed the nurse into his room. She hadn't mentioned that he was hooked up to so much shit, and he looked like he was on his death bed. I walked over to the side of the bed, and I almost didn't recognize him with the respirator over his mouth and the bruising around his face.

I leaned towards him, and as I placed my hand on his forearm, I whispered, "Max, you did good. Real good. I need you to hang in there. Don't stop fighting."

After the nurse checked his stats, she looked over to me. "I'll leave you two alone for a few minutes. They say he can hear you, so just keep talking to him, and let me know if you need anything."

Once she was gone, I looked down at Max and watched the rise and fall of his chest as the respirator filled his lungs with oxygen. It was tough seeing him so messed up, and knowing it should've been me lying there, I would've done anything to be able to trade places with him. He didn't deserve any of it, and I needed to tell him I was sorry. I'd never been one for talking. I'd always kept things bottled up, but Max could take one look at me and know what was on my mind. As much as I needed him to do that now, I knew he couldn't. So, I pulled up a chair next to him and just started talking.

"You know, I could really use some of your unsolicited advice right about now. I've made a real mess of things, and I'm not sure I have it in me to fix it. I was too caught up in getting my revenge. I needed them to pay for what they'd done, and I was too focused on them to see that the people I cared about might get caught in the crossfire. I'm sorry for that. I'm sorry you're in here fighting for your life because of the choices I made. I need you to pull through this and tell me how to fix it. I know you'd just tell me that all this comes with the territory, that I needed to toughen up and do what needs to be done, but I don't even know where to start. Hell, I've still got Lenny locked up in that damn warehouse. I've gotta deal with that shit before I can deal with the mess I've made with Tristen." I ran my fingers through my hair as I leaned back in my chair. "Hell, I've really fucked up there. I didn't mean for it to happen. I was just caught up in making her mine, and I didn't even realize what was happening until it had already happened. I thought I'd be able to keep my guard up, to protect myself from all those feelings, but she got to me, brother. She found a way through, and now, I'm all messed up in the head."

When I didn't get a response, I looked over to him and saw that he was still out cold. It was late. I needed to get Tristen home, and hopefully, by the time we made it back, he'd be awake. I stopped by to let the nurse know I was leaving, then I headed to find Tristen. When

I got to the waiting room, she was sound asleep in her chair. She'd been through hell and was beyond exhausted. I walked over and lifted her into my arms, cradling her close to my chest as I carried her out to the car. Once I had her settled inside, she mumbled, "How is he?"

"He's making it okay. Get some sleep."

In a matter of seconds, she drifted back off to sleep. She continued to sleep all the way back to the condo, and as soon as we got upstairs, she headed down the hall and went to bed. As much as I hated to leave her, especially alone and upset, I needed to get over to the warehouse and deal with Lenny. I set the alarm and headed down to my car. I was running on fumes as I headed to the warehouse, but the thought of finally getting to Lenny gave me the drive to keep going. When I walked in, Ryder was there waiting for me. When I started towards the room where I'd put Lenny, Ryder said, "Before you go in there, I think you need to have a word with Darla."

The look on his face made me curious. "Why? What's going on?"

"She's got some information you'd be interested in."

"About?"

"Just talk to her."

I left him and went straight to the room where I had her bound to the chair. As soon as I walked in, I went over and I released her from the restraints. Relief washed over her as she stood. "Are you letting me go?"

"That's up to you. Ryder says you have information for me."

"I'm not sure if it'll help… or if it even matters."

"Let me decide that."

"I told you that Lenny was in trouble with Calhoun."

"Yeah?"

"Well there's more. He has this book… like some ledger or somethin'. It has all of his transactions and shows where he's been skimming off the top. If Calhoun knew, he'd be dead already. Lenny knows it, and he knows Calhoun has become suspicious."

"So, how much money are we talking about?"

"Thousands and thousands. It started off with just a little, but he got greedy."

"Any idea where this ledger is?"

"It's in his car, hidden under the driver's seat. You have to look for it, but it's there. I've seen it myself."

"Are you sure it's still there?"

"I saw him put it there before we went to eat breakfast."

"Go outside and wait in the black truck. There's a cooler in the back. Get a drink and get inside. Stay put until Ryder comes out. Understood?"

"Understood." As she started for the door, she turned to me and asked, "What about Lenny?"

"Get to the truck, Darla."

As soon as she was gone, I left that room and

headed over to Lenny. When I walked in, he was barely conscious. His face was even more swollen than I remembered, and he was struggling to breathe. A calmness settled over me as I walked over to Lenny and placed a black sack over his head. He groaned as I pulled him to his feet. He tried to resist as I tugged him out of the room, but his fight was futile. He was beaten and weak, barely able to walk, and the inability to see only made him more helpless. I continued to lead him forward until we entered another room, a room where his life would soon come to an end. Ryder came up behind Lenny and helped me secure him to the hook with his hands over his head. When I removed the sack, his swollen eyes widened as he looked around the room.

"What is this?" he gasped. Without answering, I walked over to the table full of tools and reached for a sledgehammer. As I headed back over to Lenny, he started to shake his head and pleaded, "Don't! Just shoot me. Get this shit over with!"

"For ten years I've had to live with the fact that you not only killed my father, but you murdered Lainey and my daughter. I've had to live with that every minute of every day. Now, it's your time to feel the pain I felt all those years."

"It doesn't have to be like this! I'll give you anything you want."

"You're about to give me the only thing I've ever wanted from you. Your life in exchange for theirs."

Three hours later, I took out my phone and took a

picture of Lenny's remains. Once I'd sent it to Ryder's phone, I turned to him and said, "We need to clean up this mess, and then, you get Darla and get to Sacramento. I want that ledger and that picture in Calhoun's hands by tomorrow night."

"You got it, boss."

After we'd taken care of Lenny's body, Ryder got in the truck with Darla and headed towards California. Once they'd gone, I got in my car and started the engine. I sat there for a minute, letting the satisfaction of Lenny's death wash over me. It was done. He'd finally paid for the hell he'd put me and my family through. I thought I'd feel differently, that I would find the peace I was looking for, but there was still a storm of emotions raging inside of me. I needed time to clear my head before I headed home. My mind was bombarded with thoughts as I pulled out onto the main road and started to drive. As I thought about everything that had happened, I realized that my life had been broken into two separate worlds— the one before Tristen and the one after. Since Lainey's death, I hadn't truly lived. I'd kept myself shut off from others, holding on to my pain and my thirst for revenge alone, but that was over. Tonight, I closed the door on the world before Tristen, and I was ready to take a chance on my future.

It was well after sunrise by the time I made it home. I just wanted to get in the bed next to Tristen and forget everything. I took a hot shower and slipped into the bed next to her. Thankfully she didn't resist. Instead, she nestled her back against my chest, and as soon as I felt the warmth of her body next to mine, the tension I'd been carrying started to fade. I could feel myself drifting, knowing sleep was coming, but I fought it. I had her next to me, safe in my arms, and I didn't want to wake up only to find that it had all been just a dream.

Chapter 22
Tristen

It was time for me to decide if I was going to give up and stop fighting for something I may never have or press forward. Either way, I knew it wouldn't be easy. Walking away from him would hurt in ways I could only imagine. I loved him, and I wanted a life with him, but there were no guarantees. A man like him, damaged and stubborn as hell, would be hard to deal with, but I'd seen glimpses of the man he could be—soft and gentle, tender and caring. He was a man worth fighting for. He'd given me so much, things that I didn't even know I wanted, and yet, I found myself hoping for more. I wanted the part of him that he tried to keep hidden, the part he didn't allow others to see—his heart. As I looked at him sleeping in the bed next to me, I knew I'd do anything to get it. I wanted to help heal his broken heart, but before I could do that, I needed all the pieces. I needed him to trust me, and it was up to me to prove to him that he could.

With my mind set on what I needed to do, I got out of bed and got dressed. Knowing he'd gotten in late, I headed into the kitchen and got us both a cup of coffee. Hearing me stirring around the room, Nathan rolled over to face me and with sleepy eyes, he gave me a half smile. "Morning, Angel."

"Morning." I placed his coffee over on the bedside table and sat down on the edge of the bed. "I called the hospital, and Max hasn't come around yet. But his blood pressure is doing better, and they've taken him off the respirator."

"That sounds promising."

"I thought so, and Tony is up and doing much better."

"Good to hear." He rubbed the sleep from his eyes and then reached for his coffee. Before he took a drink, he asked, "How about you? Are you doing okay?"

"A little rough around the edges, but I'm fine." I bit my bottom lip as I tried to work up the courage to say the words. I was wavering and knew if I didn't just say it, I would lose my nerve. "You know… it isn't what happened with those men or what is going to happen to them that gets to me. It's the fact that you shut me out. It hurt me."

His brow furrowed as he propped himself up on his elbow and studied me apprehensively. "I didn't shut you out, Tristen. I was trying to protect you. This is my past… it doesn't concern you."

His words stung more than he realized, but I continued on. "See, that's where you're wrong. If this is going to work, you have to let me in… or you have to let me go."

He shook his head in frustration and stood up from the bed. He raked his hands through his hair as he paced across the room. Finally, he turned to me and said,

"Tristen, I don't want you to see that part of me."

"Nathan, don't you see… I love you regardless of your past, and I want to be a part of your future. If you feel the same about me, then this is how you show me."

After a long tense pause, he sat down on the edge of the bed. "I do feel the same."

"Good, because whether you know it or not, I love you, Nathan." I walked over to him and placed my hands on his chest. "I think I fell in love with you the night you rescued me, and since that day, you've made me fall for you over and over again. I want to be with you… not just when it's easy and everything is fine, but also when it's hard and gut-wrenchingly complicated. So, let me stand beside you, not put me behind a closed door."

I could see the wheels turning in his head as I waited for his answer. Tension rolled off him as he considered his next move. I knew it wouldn't be easy for him to talk about and I worried he'd just blow me off, but eventually, he said, "What do you want to know?"

"Everything."

With that, he started talking. He spent the next half-hour telling me everything that had happened over the past week. It was surreal hearing all the grisly details of how he'd gotten Lenny and his girlfriend to the warehouse, and how Joey had been able to find us using her cellphone. He didn't go into all the details, but he told me that he'd taken care of Lenny. The news didn't surprise me, and I couldn't blame him for killing him.

"I know that Lainey meant the world to you, that you loved her and Lila Grace, and I know they took them from you. Both of those men were cold blooded murderers, and what they did is unforgiveable. Whatever you did to him is better than he deserves."

"I can't disagree with you there." He kissed me on the forehead and said, "Are you ready to go see about our boys?"

It was clear that he was done talking, and I was good with that. He'd done what I needed him to do, so I answered, "Absolutely."

"I'm going to take a quick shower, and then we can go."

While he went to get ready, I walked to the kitchen to grab a bowl of cereal. By the time he walked in, I was almost done eating. He peered over my shoulder with a puzzled look. "What the hell is that?"

"Cereal. Duh."

"You're seriously eating Cocoa Puffs?"

"What's wrong with Cocoa Puffs?"

"Nothing… if you're twelve."

"Well, it beats that awful fiber stuff of yours. I don't know how you can stand to eat that crap. It tastes like cardboard."

"It's good for you."

"Maybe if you're eighty." I laughed as I got up and put my bowl in the sink. "Now, are you ready to go or what?"

"I'm all set."

I followed him down to the garage, and I found myself getting nervous as we started for the car. Without realizing it, I'd stopped walking, and I was standing there staring at the blood-stained concrete. Thoughts of Max lying there on the ground fighting for his life came rushing back to me. Seeing that I was upset, Nathan came up behind me and with his mouth close to my ear, he whispered, "It's going to be okay."

"You really think so?"

"There's only one way to find out." He took my hand and led me over to the car. Once I was inside, he started the car and since Tony was closer, he drove us over to check on him. As I'd hoped, he was doing much better. The bullet hadn't hit any vital organs, and if he continued to progress, they hoped to release him by the next morning. After a short visit with him, we headed to Regional to see Max. I could feel the anxiousness building inside of me as we got closer to the hospital. I hadn't gotten a good feeling when I spoke with his nurse earlier that morning, and she said he was unresponsive. By the time we made it to the hospital, I was a nervous wreck. I wasn't sure what to expect when Nathan opened the door to Max's room. When I stepped in and saw Max's bright eyes looking at me, my heart nearly leapt out of my chest.

I turned to Nathan and tried to contain my excitement as I said, "He's awake!"

"I see that." He chuckled as he walked over to the

edge of the bed. "How ya feeling?"

"I've been better," Max told him with a strained voice, "but I'm doing okay. They seem to think I'm gonna live."

"Well, that's good to hear. You had us worried there for a minute."

I walked over next to Nathan and added, "Are you really okay?"

Max gave me a smile and a quick wink. "It's gonna take more than a couple of bullets to take me down."

"Seriously, Max. It was really bad. You had us both scared to death."

Max looked over to Nathan and teased, "You were worried about me? Now, that's sweet."

"Don't be a dick, Max," Nathan scolded. "You were pretty fucked up when they loaded you into that helicopter."

"Well, it's my own damn fault. I should've double-checked the van. Hell, I should've done a lot of things."

"None of this was *your fault*," Nathan assured him.

"Well, it sure as hell isn't yours, and if you think it is, you're wrong." Max grimaced as he shifted his body in the bed. "Besides, none of that matters right now. We need to be prepared for blowback from Calhoun. Once I get my laptop, I'll get…"

"No. You're not doing a goddamn thing but laying in that fucking bed and getting better. Nothing else." Nathan shook his head. "And you can put your mind at ease over Calhoun. I've got him covered."

"How's that?"

"I said, I've got it covered. Now, you focus on you and leave the rest to me."

"If you say so." I could tell by the sound of Max's voice that he was concerned, but he knew once Nathan set his mind to something, there was no use arguing with him. "Any issues with the cops?"

"Right now they think it was just a random kidnapping attempt. We'll do what we can to keep them focused in that direction."

"If you bring my laptop over I can…."

"*Max.*"

He raised his hands in defense. "What? You can't blame a guy for trying."

In an attempt to change the subject, I asked, "Do you need anything?"

"You mean other than my laptop?" he chuckled. "No, I'm good. Anna Kate was my emergency contact, so the hospital called her this morning. She's on her way here, and I'm sure she'll take really good care of me… or finish me off. There's no way to be sure."

"I'm glad she's coming. I'd like to meet her if that's okay."

"Yeah, that'd be good. She's coming up from Seattle and planning to stay with me for a few days. I'm sure she'd like a distraction."

"Good. I look forward to it." The more he spoke, the heavier his eyelids became. He was trying to put on a show for us, but it was clear that he had a long recovery ahead of him. "I'm going to head down to the cafeteria to get a cup of coffee. Can I get you anything?"

"A cheeseburger would be good."

"I'll see what they have." I turned to Nathan and motioned him towards the door. "Why don't we let him rest a bit and grab him something to eat?"

"Sounds good. I'll meet you in the hall. I need a minute with him."

I nodded and stepped out of the room. It was several minutes before Nathan came out, and something about the look on his face told me he needed a minute before I spoke. We walked in silence to the cafeteria, and it wasn't until we got there that he said anything. "You really think getting him a burger is the best thing for him?"

"No. Definitely not. Maybe we can find some soup or something."

"Yeah, but he isn't gonna like it."

"I'm sure it will be better than what they have planned for him."

Smiling, I walked over to the counter and ordered Max's chicken noodle soup and two cups of coffee. Once it was ready, we took it upstairs and visited with him for a few more minutes. His sister was coming soon, and we both knew he needed to get some rest before she arrived, so as soon as he finished his soup, we left.

Once we left Max, we decided to go grab dinner.

Overall, it had been a good day, and it rolled into a good night. As soon as we got home, Nathan took my hand and led me into my bedroom. "Why are we coming in here?"

"It turns out I kind of like your bed."

"You do, huh?"

"It smells like you."

"If I sleep in your bed, it will smell like me, too."

"It's not the same," he told me as he pulled me close and started to nibble on the curve of my neck.

"Your bed is bigger."

"Your bed is softer." He reached for the hem of my shirt and pulled it over my head. "Just like you."

His hands slipped around my back as he unhooked my bra and let it fall to the floor. He leaned over me, covering my mouth with a hungry kiss, and everything around me seemed to slip away. The caress of his lips was magic, making me feel like I was floating on air. The tips of his fingers trailed along my spine, and I arched towards him, seeking the heat of his touch. As he continued to kiss me, I could feel a fire burning deep inside me, smoldering as it spread through my body. A rush of heat unfurled in my belly as he released my mouth and looked down at me. He stood there silently staring at me, appraising me. Everything about him seduced my senses. His touch. His smell. The way he looked at me. I'd never wanted anything like I wanted him. The way his eyes filled with lust and love when he looked at me only increased my need for him.

I reached for his shirt, unbuttoning it slowly, and I felt the muscles of his chest quiver as my fingertips brushed along his skin. As I slipped it off his shoulders, I looked up at him and whispered, "You don't have to say the words... I feel it when you touch me... and when you look at me."

His lips brushed against mine, but not gently like before. Instead, it was hot, passionate, and demanding. I gasped as he lifted me up, cradling me close to his chest as he carried me over to the bed. He held me tightly, making me feel safe in his arms. Seconds later, I was on my back with his rough, impatient hands roaming all over my body. His need was building with each kiss and each touch, and he was losing all sense of control. My breath caught as his hands slid down to my waist, and he unfastened my jeans before slowly lowering them down my hips. He trailed his hand along between my thigh and center as he moved his mouth to my breast, circling my nipple with his tongue. His other hand slid under my back, pulling me closer to his mouth as I moaned with pleasure. His every touch added fuel to the fire burning inside me.

Impatient for more, I reached for his belt, letting him know that I was just as eager as he was. I unbuckled it and set to greedily unzipping his pants before starting to tug them down. A devious smirk crossed his face as he slowly stood up, dropping his pants to the floor. He knew the effect he had on me, and as my eyes moved to his growing erection inside his boxer briefs, I couldn't help but lick my lips. His blue eyes darkened as he slowly, tantalizingly freed himself from them before kicking them to the side. He stood naked before me, letting my heated gaze wash over him as he took his thick length in his hand. Desire pooled inside me as I watched with rapt attention and started to squirm impatiently. Heat rushed through me as my eyes roamed over his perfectly defined abs and pronounced V. He was beautiful, and he was mine. As I watched him, I cupped my breasts in my palms before trailing one of my hands down my stomach and between my legs. I touched myself for a moment, circling my clit with my fingertip, emboldened by his lust-filled eyes following my every movement. As a little moan escaped my body, his lips parted, and he whispered, "Fuck."

When I couldn't wait a moment longer, I looked up at him and pleaded, "Show me how much you want me. Please, Nathan."

A deep growl vibrated through his chest as he lowered himself onto the bed and settled between my legs. He brushed against my center, teasing me relentlessly before he finally thrust deep inside me. My head fell back as I gasped for air, my fingernails digging into his back, and my entire body gripped with heat.

He moved slowly, meticulously at first, but then his pace quickened, becoming more demanding and intense with each roll of his hips. The muscles inside me began to tighten as my legs drew up beside him. My hands curled around his ass as I held on to him, bracing myself for the wave of pleasure that I could feel growing inside me. His steady rhythm never faltered, until we both reached our climax. He lowered himself on top of me with the heat of his breath at my neck, and he didn't move. He just lay there, holding me close. I loved the feeling of his body on mine. When I was in his arms, I could pretend that he'd given me the one thing I truly wanted, but deep down, I knew the truth. I didn't have his heart, not the way that I'd always wanted. And I was beginning to worry that I never would.

Chapter 23
Nitro

I felt it right along with her—every spark, every flicker. It was impossible to ignore. I'd tried to fight it, to pretend it wasn't happening, but I couldn't deny that she was getting to me. As much as I wanted to be in the moment with her and give her all I had to give, I could feel a part of me holding back. I let myself fall asleep in her arms, but the next morning, I got up out of the bed long before she ever woke up. I left her a note saying I had to go into the office, which wasn't exactly a lie. I needed to touch base with Ryder and make sure everything with Calhoun had been handled. Before I called him, I decided to drive over and see Mom. It was early when I got there, and I had worried I might wake her, but she was already in the kitchen making coffee and toast.

"Well, hi there, stranger." She walked over to me and gave me a big hug and a kiss on the cheek. "I was beginning to think you'd forgotten about me."

"Now, you know that could never happen."

"Well, you haven't called, and I haven't seen hide nor hair of you since the night you brought Tristen by." I sat down at the table while she got us both some toast. "I've seen lots of Murray... way too much of Murray. I think something's going on with him."

"I was out of town and asked him to keep an eye on you until I got back."

"It would've been nice to know what was going on. He had me worried that something had happened."

"Everything is fine." I considered telling her about Lenny and Joey, but I decided against it. I knew how she felt. She'd made that clear years ago when Murray and I were trying to find them. She wanted us to leave it alone, that enough loss had occurred, but I didn't feel the same. Trying to reassure her, I continued, "It's just been a busy week."

"I really liked Tristen. I think there's something special about her."

"She liked you, too."

"I think this girl is the one," she pushed.

I shook my head and said, "Don't start, Mom."

"I saw the way you looked at her."

"*Mother.*"

Ignoring me, she stood up and walked out of the kitchen. A few minutes later, she came back with a photograph in her hand. She looked down at me and said, "I've been thinking about something since that night…. I want you to look at this."

I took the picture in my hand and was surprised to see it was an old photograph of Lainey and I standing outside our old house. "Why are you showing me this now?"

"Because I want you to look at it… really look at it." I looked down at Lainey for a moment, then dropped the picture down on the table. She quickly picked it back up and held it in front of me. "No, I don't want you to just look at her... I want you to look at yourself, Nathan. Look at the man in that picture... see the smile on his face... the love in his eyes when he looks at that girl."

"I don't see what your point is in all this."

"You were happy, really happy." Tears filled her eyes as she placed her hand on my shoulder.

"They were everything to me."

"I know that, and I'm not asking you to close the book on what you had with Lainey. I'm just asking you to *not be afraid* to turn the page. Lainey would want you to move on, so stop letting fear keep you from finding happiness."

"I've never considered myself a fearful person, Mom." I ran my hands through my hair with frustration. "You don't do the things I do when you're afraid."

"You're wrong. You're the most controlling person I know. You feel like you have to micromanage every aspect of your life because you're afraid something bad will happen if you don't." With the picture of Lainey and me still in her hand, she sat down next to me. "No one could blame you for feeling that way, but this is no way to live."

"What am I supposed to do?"

"You have to open your heart to Tristen and let her love you."

"It's not that easy."

"But it is. I'm not asking you to do the impossible." She placed her hand on my arm and gave me a light squeeze. "You just have to be brave enough to love her back. Don't be afraid to be happy."

I looked down at the picture and took note of the goofy grin on my face. She was right. I was happy back then. I felt love without limits, gave it without second thoughts, and lived, truly lived. I took the picture and put it in my back pocket, gave Mom a hug, and headed out to my car. When I left there, I just started driving with no real destination in mind. I drove out to the Cape where I had taken Tristen a few weeks back. When I thought back to that day, how beautiful she looked and how good I felt with her, it was hard not to smile. She had a way of making everything better. I pulled off the trail and headed out to the restaurant where we'd eaten lunch. I'd just pulled into the parking lot, when I got a text message from Ryder.

Ryder:
Found the log.

Me:
Good

Ryder:
Darla helped find Calhoun.

Damaged Goods

Me:

And?

Ryder:

Just made the delivery.

Me:

Well done. You headed to your sister's?

Ryder:

Got myself an invite to dinner- gonna see where that goes first.

Me:

Darla?

Ryder:

The one and only. I'll be back tomorrow.

Me:

Watch yourself with that one.

Ryder:

Always.

I wasn't surprised that he was making a play for Darla. He and I both knew it wouldn't go anywhere, but he was young and just didn't give a shit. After I put my phone in my pocket, I went into the Seafood Shack and

L. Wilder

sat down at one of the corner booths. It wasn't long before Dottie came over and took my order. Once she brought my food, I ate a few bites and decided I was too preoccupied to eat. I tossed a couple of twenties on the table and waved to Dottie on my way out the door. With my mind on everything my mother had said, I got back in my car, and an hour later, I found myself parked at the curb of the cemetery. I sat there staring for several minutes before I finally forced my hand to move towards the door and open it.

I walked over and knelt at Lainey's headstone, placing the palm of my hand on her name. "It's me... I know it's been a while since I came to see you. It doesn't mean you haven't been on my mind, because you have.... I think about you and Lila Grace every day." Trailing the lines of her name with the tip of my finger, I continued. "I got them, Lainey. It took a long time, but I kept my word, and I got them." I let out a deep sigh as I stood up and looked around the cemetery. "It's finally over."

I told her about Colton and his upcoming marriage. I rattled on for several minutes, but I still hadn't said what I needed to say. I took a minute to collect my thoughts, then continued, "I've been doing a lot of thinking, and I want to thank you, Lainey. You taught me how to love.... You showed me just how good life can be. I haven't let myself have that for a long time. I've been too afraid to take a chance. It damn near killed me when I lost you and Lila Grace. I loved you both so much. I still do. I didn't think I had it in me to love like that again, and I was scared to take another hit. I was scared to lose it again. But I've met someone. She's really something, Lainey. You'd like her. She is tough, and like you, she doesn't let me get away with any shit. She's smart, beautiful, and she makes me want to be better."

I ran my hands down my face as I tried to swallow the emotions that were creeping up my throat. "I know there's no guarantees... I don't have a way to look into the future, but something in my gut tells me she's worth the risk. I love you, Lainey. But I have to let you go, so I can love her the way she deserves."

With that, I turned and went back to my car. I drove over to the office to check in with Murray, and told him about my concerns about Calhoun. I wanted to believe that the score would be settled and there wouldn't be any repercussions to us taking out Joey, but there was no way to tell for sure. Even though he didn't think we had anything to worry about, he assured me that he'd have the guys keep an eye on things. Once he'd gone for the day, I closed out a few accounts, and then headed back to the condo. By the time I got there, it was well after dark, and when I went to look for Tristen, I found her soaking in a hot bath. She was covered from head to toe in bubbles and reminded me of a kid when she looked up at me and smiled. As she motioned me over towards the tub, she called out, "Hey there, handsome. Come on over and join me."

I didn't miss the spark of desire that flashed through her eyes as I started to remove my clothes. Like a predator waiting to pounce on its prey, she watched each piece of clothing drop to the floor. My girl had a craving for my cock, and I was more than willing to satisfy her hunger. She shifted forward, giving me room to ease in behind her, and once I was settled, she leaned her back against my chest. "You left early this morning."

I kissed her on the shoulder as I reached for her sponge and started washing her back. "Sorry about that. I had some things to tend to."

"Have you heard from Ryder?"

"He's fine."

"Did everything go okay with him and Darla?"

"You could say that." I snickered. "He's having dinner with Darla tonight."

"Really? I thought Lenny was her boyfriend or something."

"He was."

"Then, what is she doing hooking up with Ryder? Shouldn't there be some kind of mourning period after something like this?"

I chuckled under my breath. "Maybe she needs a shoulder to cry on."

"Maybe so." She sighed. "I'm sure Ryder can take care of himself."

"I'm sure he can."

"So, you think everything is going to be okay with

that man you were talking to him about?"

"Calhoun?" She nodded as I poured more soap onto the palm of my hand and ran it down her shoulders and arms. "No way to be sure, but I figure he'll think we did him a favor."

She fell silent as I started to wash along her collarbone and neck, then down to her breast. Her head tilted back as my thumb brushed against her nipple, caressing it softly as I nipped and sucked along her neck under her ear. A little whimper escaped her throat as my hand trailed down her abdomen and slid between her legs. Her hips rolled forward as my fingers trailed across her clit. I loved how her body responded to my touch. Hearing her little moans and sighs only made me want her even more. Her ass slid against my growing erection, and I groaned in response. I slid my fingertips inside her and had just begun to stroke her when she moaned, "Oh god, Nathan…." Hearing my name on her lips drove me wild, and I knew I couldn't wait any longer to have her. Before she could protest, I withdrew my fingers and moved my hands to her hips, lifting her against me. Her legs spread wide as I centered her over my cock. Her back arched against me as she took one of my hands in hers and placed it over her breast. She took my other hand and held it steady on her hip as she slowly lowered herself onto me. A moan vibrated through her as she leaned her neck back against my shoulder and began to grind her hips into mine. With one hand, I took her slick breast in my palm, gently sliding my fingertips around her nipple, teasing her with each squeeze. With my other, I held on to her hip as I began thrusting in tandem with hers. Her hands gripped the sides of the tub as she began to pant and rock faster, enjoying the onslaught of sensations I was giving her. As she pushed against me, my palm slid from her hip down to her clit, slipping easily over her skin.

As I began to stroke her with a tormenting rhythm, she cried out in pleasure. Her thrusts became more forceful as she took me deeper and deeper, and I could feel her muscles contracting all around me. My body was taut as I struggled to hold back my climax. Her body felt so good, so right, but I wanted to give her the most intense pleasure she'd ever experienced. As she began to tremble around me, I heard her breath quivering with anticipation and need. I slid both of my hands to her hips and held on as her orgasm approached. Her hips rocked against mine, faster and faster in a feverish rhythm, until at last she let out a tortured groan and clamped down around my cock. My fingers dug into her hips as I pulled her down hard and came deep inside her. She collapsed back onto me, and we didn't move as the aftershocks of her orgasm rolled through her. I stayed inside her as we panted for breath and waited for our heartbeats to slow. I kissed her neck as I whispered, "Damn, woman. I don't think I'll ever get enough of you."

I was on my way to grab some clothes out of my room, when I spotted it. I took it in my hands and carried it into the living room. After I got the hammer and some nails, I went over to the fireplace and eyeballed the perfect spot for the nail. Even though I was trying to be quiet, the hammering caught her attention. She came into the room with a puzzled look on her face.

"What in the world are you doing?" She was wearing her father's t-shirt, and her hair was still damp and down around her shoulders. "It sounds like you're about to bang right through the wall."

I was standing on a chair in front of the fireplace with a hammer in my hand as I answered, "Nothing."

"Well, it certainly doesn't look like nothing."

I reached down at my feet and took the picture in my hand. After I positioned it in the center of the wall, I stepped down off the chair and took a look at it. "Looks pretty good, don't you think?"

I turned back to look at her and noticed the tears in her eyes. "But I didn't think you even liked that picture."

"I never said that." Her eyes never left the painting as I walked over to her. "I actually really like it."

"*Okay*." She answered, sounding unsure of herself. "But you said…"

"I know what I said."

"Then, what's changed?"

"Everything." I placed my hands around her waist, closing the gap between us. "You made me realize that I wasn't exactly being honest with you or myself. I do believe in love... All of it. The good and the bad."

"What are you saying?"

"I'm saying it isn't all bullshit... Love is kind. Love is patient. It protects, it trusts, and it always perseveres. I do believe in love, and most of all, I believe in you." I lowered my mouth to hers, kissing her softly. "I love you, Tristen Carmichael. Heart and soul."

"I love you, too. So very much." She looked up at the picture and smiled. "You did good. It looks great there."

"I'm glad you like it, because like me, you're stuck with it."

Nitro

Four Years Later

"Are you sure you're okay with this?" Tristen asked for the third time.

"Already told you I've got it covered."

"But you know how she can get when she's not feeling well, and you have…."

"Tristen, get to class. I have this under control." I gave her a kiss on the lips and then headed for the refrigerator. "And don't text me every five minutes to check on things."

With a disgruntled sigh, she walked over to Callie and gave her a kiss on the top of her head. "Be good for your daddy. You know how he can get when things don't go his way."

"Daddy's a bad boy," Callie replied.

"No, your daddy is a good boy. It's your mother who's bad," I told our two-year-old daughter as I walked over to the table with her bowl of cereal. "If she doesn't go on to school, she won't graduate next week."

"Go momma. You get in trouble."

Tristen kissed her one last time and then walked over to me. "Call me if you need anything."

"I won't." I gave her a quick kiss and then motioned her towards the door. "You're going to be late."

"I'll be back in a couple of hours."

"Take your time. My girl and I have big plans for the morning." I gave it my all, but I could still see the apprehension on her face as she walked towards the door.

"Don't forget to give her the pink medicine as soon as she's done eating."

"Got it."

As she opened the door, she turned to me and smiled. "And one more thing."

"Yeah?"

"I love you."

"Love you, too. Now, move your ass."

Once she was gone, I sat down at the table next to my beautiful daughter with her curly blonde hair and crystal blue eyes and smiled as she shoved a handful of cereal into her mouth. Life was good. I had everything I'd ever wanted and more. I'd never admit it to her, but I owed it to my mother. Until she said it out loud, I hadn't realized how much I was letting my fear dictate my life—not just with Tristen, but in every facet of my life. I still had my moments when I wanted to fight for control, to hold those that I cared about close and protect them at all costs, but I was slowly learning there was nothing I could do to stop the world from turning. I had to grab life by the horns and live, and with Tristen by my side, it was one hell of a ride.

"I need a dink."

I loved the sound of her sweet voice. "What do you want to drink, sweetheart?"

"Duice."

"Juice?"

"Yes, p'ease."

I got up and walked over to the fridge and filled her sippy cup with orange juice. I walked back over and sat it down on her tray. "There you go."

She reached for her cup and took a drink, and her face scrunched up like she'd tasted something awful. As she shook her head, she tossed the cup across the floor. "Yuck."

"Whoa. What was that?" I walked over and picked up the cup, then placed it back on her tray. "That wasn't nice, Callie."

"I need a dink."

"I got you a drink."

"Not good dink. Yuck."

She picked the cup up again and tossed it on the floor. Like her mother, my daughter had a fiery side, and when she didn't feel well, she was quite the little stinker. I walked over to her high chair and lifted her out of her seat. "That's enough of that."

When I kissed her on the top of her head, she was warm, and I realized that her fever was back. I took her into the kitchen and sat her down on the counter while I got her medicine out of the cabinet. "Momma said da pink bottle."

"I know you need the pink medicine, Bossy, but you need Tylenol, too."

She pouted as she shook her head. "It 'dastes bad."

"No, this is the good one. It tastes like grape."

"You sw-ure?"

"Yep. You'll like it."

Once I'd given her a teaspoon from both bottles, I carried her into the living room and sat down in my recliner. I turned on some cartoons and started rocking her. She nestled herself in the crook of my arm as her focus locked on the television screen. The more I rocked, the heavier her eyelids became, and after just a few minutes, she fell asleep in my arms. There'd been a time when I thought I'd never have it again, but at that moment, I felt complete and utter happiness.

I hadn't realized I'd dozed off, until I felt Callie tugging on the collar of my shirt. "Momma home."

I looked up and found Tristen staring down at me with a look—one that said 'I love you' without saying the words. "That was quick."

"Not really… I've been gone two hours."

"Time flies when you're having fun."

"Um hmm." She smiled excitedly. "I've got good news."

I pulled her down into my lap next to Callie and said, "Let's hear it."

"When I turned in my final today, the professor asked to talk to me after class. He told me about a job opening at the counseling center downtown. He's already put a call into the office and told them about me. He thinks I'd be perfect for the job."

"That's awesome."

"I'm just not sure if it's the right thing for me to do… under the circumstances."

"What circumstances?"

"Well, with the baby coming, I hate to start a new job, only to have to leave them in the lurch after seven or eight months."

"Wait… what?"

She bit at her lip as she took Callie from me and cradled her close to her chest. "It looks like our little Callie is going to be a big sister soon."

She looked over to me and smiled, knowing I was about to lose it. "You're pregnant?"

"Yes, Nathan. It looks like you're going to be a father… again."

"You're pregnant?" Her smile grew wider as I finally started to comprehend what she was saying. "Like, right now… right this minute… you're pregnant?"

"Yes." She placed the palm of her hand on my cheek. "I'm pregnant… right now… right this minute."

Unable to control myself, I stood up with both of them in my arms. Holding them tightly, I smiled and said, "It just keeps getting better and better."

Tristen looked up at me and said, "I love you, Nathan James."

"And I love you, Tristen James. Heart and soul."

The End.
More from Max coming soon.

Acknowledgements

Amanda Faulkner – Thank you for being an amazing PA. You support and kindness means the world to me. I don't know what I'd do without you.

Natalie Weston – I love you, chick. Even when I'm at my worst, you have a way of making me smile. Thanks for all that you do. It means so much.

Daryl and Sue Banner, The Dynamic Duo – Thank you both for making my book the best it can be. I love you both!
*If you haven't checked out Daryl Banner's books on Amazon, you are missing out. Be sure to check out his books: http://www.amazon.com/author/darylbanner

Brooke Asher – Welcome back to the crazy world of L. Wilder! Thanks for all your help with everything. You are an amazing friend, and I can't thank you enough.

Tempting Illustrations – Thank you for your amazing teasers. I loved them all! If you're looking for some amazing teasers, be sure to check them out. http://www.temptingillustrations.com

Danielle Palumbo – You simply amaze me. I can't begin to tell you how much I appreciate your support, even when it isn't easily given. You are simply awesome!

Lisa Cullinan – I truly appreciate your help, and your friendship means so much to me. You rock, lady!

Neringa Neringiukas – I can't thank you enough for sharing my book and teasers, and all of your kind words of support. Your friendship and kindness means so much to me. Thanks for being awesome.

Whynter Raven – Thanks for posting for me! You rock!

Tanya Skaggs, Sabra Browning Baroski, Donna Parrot, and Grace Heart – Thank you for reading Nitro early and helping me make it even better. You guys rock! Tanya- you are such a sweetheart. Thanks for keeping me sane.

Ana Rosso – My young Jedi. Thank you for keeping me on track, even when life tends to get in the way. I am so proud of you for writing your first book, Reaper's Creed MC. I can't wait to see what you come up with next. Keep writing!!
https://www.amazon.com/Reapers-Creed-MCDamons-Salvation-ebook/dp/B01HG1G6PS

Damaged Goods

Patricia Ann Blevins, Kaci Stewart, Danielle Deraney Palumbo, Tanya Skaggs, Terra Oenning, Sarah Hooks, Michelle Booklover, Sarah O'Rouke, Hannah Myers, and Donna Parrott – (so glad I finally got meet some of you at the signing. Love you all!) – Thank you so much for always being there with your kind words and support. Your reviews and suggestions mean the world to me. Your stories and words of encouragement always make me smile. Thanks so much for sharing them with me.

Wilder's Women – I am always amazed at how much you do to help promote my books and show your support. Thank you for being a part of this journey with me. I read all of your reviews and see all of your posts, and they mean so much to me. Love you big!

A Special Thanks to Mom – Thank you for always being there to read, chapter by chapter, giving me your complete support. You are such an amazing person, and I am honored to call you my mom.

Continue for an excerpt of Big: Book 6 in the Satan's Fury MC Series

Satan's Fury MC

Book 6

(An Excerpt)

Prologue
Mike

"Well, look who we have here," Baker snickered as he sauntered into the room with several of his hood rats following close behind.

My eyes skirted over to him and my chest tightened into a knot as I watched them file into the room. Baker was a big brute, weighing around two sixty with muscles protruding through his orange jumpsuit, while I was a tall, puny fucker who weighed a buck fifty with boots on. I was scared out of my damned mind, and rightly so. I knew what was coming. I'd seen it too many times to count, and I knew there was nothing I could do to stop it. I was stuck. I hated that feeling of helplessness and had always done my best to avoid it at all costs. I thought if I just kept my mouth shut and avoided all the roughnecks, I would be able to stay off their radar. But keeping off the grid in a place like this was damn near impossible. The GH Juvenile Detention Center was no place for a kid like me, but like a line of dominoes, the choices I'd made had landed me behind bars. I thought I was slick, that I wouldn't get caught, but I was wrong. I was wrong about a lot of damned things, and it's one of the reasons I'd found myself in the boys' bathroom surrounded by a pack of hungry wolves.

"You think you're so fucking smart. You walk around here acting like you're better than everyone else, but you ain't shit!" Baker snarled.

Baker was a grade A asshole, and over his stint in juvie, he'd acquired quite a following. He and his cronies had a thing for fucking with anyone who was smaller or weaker than them, and with my scrawny ass, there was no doubt I was an easy target. He stood there glaring at me like some rabid dog, and I knew he had his mind set on annihilating me. I felt the walls closing in as I looked towards the door. My fight or flight instincts kicked in and I felt an overwhelming urge to get the hell out of there, but a couple of his goons were guarding the exit. There was no way out. Knowing I was cornered, Baker's lips curled into a cold, heartless smile. There was no honor in fights like this. No code. It was simply the survival of the fittest, and I was damned from the start.

I swallowed hard and muttered, "I don't want any trouble, Baker."

"Nobody asked you what you wanted, you fucking pussy," he barked as he slammed his fist into my gut. Before I had a chance to defend myself, he reared back and punched me again right in the damn nose. Tears filled my eyes as I stumbled and fell flat on my face. As soon as my limp body hit the floor, he started kicking me in my side and abdomen causing me to curl into a protective ball. Bile burned at the back of my throat and the stench of piss and body odor only made it harder to resist the urge to puke. Laughter filled the room as I tried unsuccessfully to lift myself off the ground. Wobbling like a ninety-year-old heart patient, I didn't get very far. My arms felt like lead weights and my legs were quivering from the pain, making it impossible to move.

"We gotta get the hell out of here. The guards are gonna come looking for us," one of the guys urged. Their sneakers squeaked against the cold, concrete floor as they paced nervously back and forth. They were getting anxious, and I prayed they'd convince him to leave.

"We've got time. They're dealing with Duncan," Baker snickered. "Besides, I'm not done with our little computer freak just yet."

Baker was right. Duncan, one of the more emotionally disturbed kids in our hall, had one of his meltdowns, and it would take them all to get him settled back down. They wouldn't be coming anytime soon, and my hopes of someone coming to my rescue were completely squashed.

"I'm done with this bullshit. He'd not worth the trouble," one of them grumbled as he walked out the door.

"I knew you were a pussy, but I thought you'd at least put up a fight." Baker gave me a shove with his foot and snickered. "Come on, douchebag. Get up."

I was down, but I wasn't completely out. His words

were like a spark, fueling the fire that burned deep inside me. I couldn't give up—not just yet. Bruised and winded, I mustered the strength to stand. Anger exploded within me as I shouted, "Fuck you, Baker."

I held my breath as I took a swing at him. Satisfaction shot through me when the contact made his head jerk back. I'd thought I'd gotten him good, but my sense of pride was short-lived as his balled fist collided with my cheekbone. Everything went blurry, and I lost my footing. In a matter of seconds, my face was planted back on the bathroom floor. It was pathetic.

Baker lowered himself down on top of me and brought his mouth over to my ear. He whispered in a raw, guttural voice, "Is that all you got, pussy?"

I struggled against him, shooting my left leg out as I tried to get him off me, but I just wasn't strong enough. His hands moved up to my neck, wrapping tightly around my throat as he spat, "Where ya trying to run off to, freak-show? I'm not done with you yet."

I felt him reach into his back pocket and froze when I heard one of the guys yelp, "Don't Baker. You taking this too far."

"Shut your fucking mouth, Smith. I'll decide how far this thing goes!"

I twisted and turned, trying my best to buck him off me, but he just pressed his weight down on my body, pinning me against the concrete floor.

"Don't," I pleaded. "Just let me go. I'll keep my mouth shut. Just let me go."

"Oh, you'll keep your fucking mouth shut or I'll finish what I started."

A burning sensation rushed through my side as the blade sank deep into my lower abdomen. He twisted the knife in his hand while sinking it deeper and deeper into my flesh. I tried to hold back my cries, but the pain was too much. My screams echoed through the concrete walls, causing everyone to scatter like flies. I lay there feeling my life drain from my body, and it was in that moment that I decided I'd never be the victim again.

It took some work, but I kept the promise I'd made to myself that day. As soon as I got out of the infirmary, the guards put me in solitary for the rest of my stint in juvie. Since they had no clue who had gotten to me, the counselors said I would be safer there. Once my wounds had healed and I was back on my feet, I started working out – hours upon hours of push-ups and squats, along with any other damned exercise I could come up with in the confines of that little room. One of the guards noticed what I was up to, and thinking it would be good for me, he gave me access to the weight room when no one else was around. When I walked out of that detention center six months later, I'd gained the muscle I was after, and that's when I realized Baker actually had done me a favor.

It was only two years later when I found myself behind bars for the second time, only now, I was six-foot-four and two hundred and seventy pounds of muscle. I was stronger, mentally and physically, but that didn't mean the guys didn't try to fuck with me. It was no secret why I'd been locked up. I was different, knew things these men didn't understand, and they sure as fuck didn't like it. Computer hacking wasn't exactly a crime a typical thug understood, and the unknown brought a level of fear, a fear I learned to use to my advantage.

It was after dinner, and I was heading back to my cell when my attention was drawn over to the cell next to mine. It was Jacob's cell, the only person I ever really talked to in this joint. He was a decent guy – for a gun trafficking murderer – and talking to him helped pass the time. When I stepped inside the cell, Tank, one of the Hispanic gang members, had Jacob pinned to the wall with his fingers wound tightly around his neck. I knew I didn't need any more violations added to my record, but there was no way I was going to let him fuck with Jacob.

I stepped closer and growled, "Drop him."

Without loosening his gripe, Tank turned to me and spat, "This isn't your fight, asshole. Get the fuck out."

"Not leaving until you let him go." I looked over at Jacob, and though he'd never admit it, he was struggling. The veins in his neck were bulging, and even through all his tattoos, I could see that his face was turning blue. "Now, Tank."

His eyes glaring with anger, he snarled, "You just signed your own death sentence, motherfucker."

I took a step forward and slammed my fist into his

ribcage over and over until he dropped his hold on Jacob. I reared back my closed fist and slammed it into the side of his jaw, causing him to lose his balance and fall back against the cot. He shook his head, trying to shake off the confusion, but I didn't give him that chance. I grabbed him by the neck, squeezing him tightly around the throat like he'd done Jacob and said, "This is over, Tank. You wanna know why it's over?" When he didn't answer, I continued. "Because if you even look in his direction, I will *end you*. I'll beat the goddamned life right out of you, make you beg for me to just let you die, and then I'll fuck with you in ways you can't even begin to imagine. And not just you, Santiago Rodrigues from Fallbrook, California. I will fuck with everyone you have ever known or cared about, and you'll never even see me coming. Got me?"

He nodded, and as soon as I released him, he scurried out of the cell like a wounded rat.

I turned to Jacob. "You wanna tell me what that was all about?"

"Nope."

"Didn't think so."

As I started back towards my cell, Jacob called, "Yo, Big."

"Yeah?"

"You're supposed to be getting out next week, right?"

"That's what they've been telling me."

"You headed back home when you're released?"

My mind involuntarily drifted back to my father. He'd always held on to the hope that I'd give up computers and hacking, that I'd find a new focus. I tried, but nothing could surpass the thrill I got from sitting behind that screen. I got a high from pushing limits, ignoring boundaries, and succeeding at things no one else could. It was my obsession, and I was getting better with every click of my keyboard. Unfortunately, I wasn't the only one getting better. The world of technology was changing and becoming harder to crack, and one mistake would cost more than it ever had before. My father knew the risks and warned me about them time and time again. After I was arrested the second time, he'd made it clear that I wasn't welcome back home. He was done trying to make me different.

"Nope. Nothing there for me."

"You should head up to Clallam County. Got some friends there you should meet. I think they could use a guy like you."

"A guy like me?"

"You and your particular skill set might come in handy, but it will be up to you to convince them of that."

"And why would I do that?"

"You're just gonna have to trust me on this one. Go out on Highway 61 and turn left at the fork on Millbrook Road. Drive about five miles and you'll see an old warehouse off on the left. Pull up to the gate and ask for Cotton. Tell him Nitro sent ya."

Chapter 1

"Hey, Big." Wren smiled as she peaked her head inside my room. "Would you mind helping me with something?"

"Sure." Wren is Stitch's old lady. Some would say they are an unlikely match, but I disagree. Wren had a way about her. Without even trying, she could break through the walls we put up and see the good that lies behind them. Stitch is one of the toughest guys I know. He's downright intimidating at times, but he's always been willing to do anything to protect the people he cares about. Wren saw past his rough exterior and found the heart hidden beneath. She and Wyatt, and now Mia, have been the best thing that ever happened to him. "Whatcha got?"

"It's Wyatt. He's trying to hook up his new game system in the family room, and he isn't having much luck. I don't have a clue how to do it, so…"

I stood up from my computer and walked over to her. Mia was sleeping soundly in the crook of her arm. She was all dolled up in one of those soft pink outfits with a little pink beanie on her head. Hard to believe Stitch's kid could be so damn cute.

"I'll get him fixed up."

Relief washed over her as she said, "I'd appreciate

it. He wants to have it ready when Dusty gets here, otherwise I wouldn't have bothered you."

"Not a problem."

I followed her out into the hall and down to the family room. When we walked in, Wyatt had cords and remotes scattered all over the room. From the scowl on his face, I could see that he was getting frustrated. He bit at his bottom lip as he tried to force the HDMI cable into the side of the TV, and I had to swallow my smile. I'd always seen a lot of myself in Wyatt, knowing his brain worked differently than most, and I understood his aggravation. Like me, he wanted to get it right the first time. "Need a hand?"

"I can get it," he grumbled.

"I'm sure you can." I walked over to the coffee table and picked up the box with his new PlayStation and said, "I've been wanting to check this out for weeks. Stitch get this for you?"

Without looking in my direction, he answered, "Yes, sir. Made all A's on my report card."

Wren smiled with pride as she said, "He was the only one in his class."

"All A's. That's pretty impressive, dude."

He let out a sigh as he turned towards me and offered me the cable. "Can you do this? I can't get it to go in."

I took it from his hand and slid it into the correct slot. Together, we took the remaining parts out of the box and in a matter of minutes, we had it all up and running. Wyatt and I settled ourselves on the large, L-shaped sofa and started playing *Call of Duty*. We were both lost in the game when Wren asked, "Hey, Big. Have you heard from Tristen?"

"Not since she left." She'd gone to Mexico with one of her girlfriends for a couple of days. We all understood why she needed a break from the club. She had a thing for Smokey, and while we all knew he didn't feel the same – including Tristen – it hurt her when he fell for MJ.

"I thought they were supposed to be back yesterday."

"You know how things go in Mexico. Maybe they just decided to stay a little longer."

"Maybe," she answered in a low, concerned voice.

"I'm sure she's fine. If we haven't heard from her by tomorrow, I'll check on her," I offered.

"You're right. I'm sure she's okay."

"There a reason why you needed her?"

She looked down at Mia cradled in her arms. "I just wanted to see if she could watch Wyatt while we went for the baby's checkup."

"I can keep an eye on him."

"Are you sure?"

I gave Wyatt a little nudge with my elbow as I said, "Gotta figure out how to beat him at this game. Figure it's gonna take a while."

"That would be great. I'll be back in a couple of hours, and if you need anything, just call."

"Take your time," I told her as I tried to return my focus to the game. I was surprised to see that Wyatt was already two kills ahead of me. "Damn, dude. You're good at this."

Never losing his focus, he fired off several rounds against the enemy. "You can catch up. Make your advance, stay covered, and change your weapon. That one is for girls."

"Is that right?"

"I thought you knew that kind of stuff," Wyatt taunted.

"Guess I still have a lot to learn." I laughed as I switched to my secondary and tried to catch up to him. We hadn't been playing long when Dusty came in. Needless to say, I lost my spot on the sofa and the boys quickly forgot I was even in the room. I sat back in the recliner and smiled as I watched them play. They were good together—two little amigos that had found a friendship that would last them a lifetime.

Once Wren returned from the baby's appointment, I went back to my room and got to work. Over the past few months, I'd been busy. The demand for weapons was continuing to increase, and in order to keep up, the club had to make some changes. We'd done well with our shipments in the past, managed to stay under that ATF's radar, but with the increase in deliveries, it would be harder to stay that way. It was time for us to start buying the parts separately, which would make it easier to ship them without detection and leave the full assembly to be done once they reached Mexico. It was up to me to check out Nitro's new contacts and make sure they didn't have any skeletons lurking in the closet. He had his own people for this sort of thing, but he wanted me to be there to double check their findings. Nitro wasn't a man who took chances, and that's why Cotton used him. Over the years, we'd established an understanding. We all knew in our line of work there were high expectations and the failure to bring results would bring consequences that threatened to pull us under.

I'd gone through the first guy with no real red flags, but the second was a different story. I knew right away something was up with him. I picked up my phone and called Nitro. As soon as he answered, I blurted, "You've gotta be fucking kidding me?"

"About?"

"Claybrooks."

"You mean the cop?"

"Damn. You had me worried there for a minute." We'd had our run-ins with cops in the past, each one thinking he'd found his way inside, but none had ever made it very far. It was evident that Claybrooks was working an undercover op, and it wasn't like Nitro not to smell him from a mile away.

"Yeah, I thought you could have a little fun with him," Nitro snickered. "Give him something to occupy his time for a while."

"You want me to bury him?"

"Make an impression."

"You got it."

As soon as I hung up the phone, I started working on Mr. Jonathan Claybrooks, aka Detective David Keen. I sent a phishing email requesting to run an update on his computer's security, and within the hour, he'd responded with everything I needed—his password, home address, pin, email addresses, and his social. Once I had that information, there was nothing I couldn't do. I started with his email contacts, sending evidence of misconduct to his commanding officer and the mayor. It would only be a matter of time before he'd lose his job, but that wasn't enough. Before I closed out his email, I sent a malicious virus to everyone on his contact list, making sure they all knew he was behind the destruction of their own personal security. I reported his car stolen, triggering his vehicle's security system to send a remote signal that blocked the engine from starting. Then, I moved on to his bank accounts, completely clearing his checking and savings accounts. After I had his cell phone and utilities shut off, I attacked his social media, slamming his Facebook, Twitter, and Instagram pages with goat porn and golden showers, along with photoshopped pics of him wearing KKK t-shirts and hats – just enough to leave a lasting impression on everyone who knew him. Finally, just for fun, I changed all his passwords and added a required updated pin to each, making it frustrating as hell for him to regain access to any of his accounts.

Big

I leaned back in my chair and stared at the computer screen with a sense of satisfaction, knowing that I'd just yanked the rug out from underneath Keen. Sure, there was the possibility that over time he could convince people that he'd been hacked and get his life back, but the damage had been done. That element of doubt would always be there, leaving a lasting scar on his reputation. Every time he picked up his phone, each time he logged into his computer or used his debit card, he would remember this day and the panic he'd felt. After today, Keen and all those detective pricks would think twice before they fucked with Nitro again. I was just about to add his name to the possible American terrorist list, FAA No-Fly, and DHS Homegrown, when there was a knock on my door.

"Yo, Big Mike." Q' stuck his head inside. "You heard anything about Tristen? Some chick keeps calling the bar. Says she's been trying to call her cell but can't get her to answer."

Hearing her name for the second time that day gave me an uneasy feeling. Tristen had been with the club for just over a year. At first, she was just one of the hang arounds, looking for a good time with no real connection to any of the guys, but over time, she started to make herself useful. She did what she could to help around the bar and in the kitchen, and it didn't go unnoticed. When Cotton found out she was a runaway, he hired her and set her up in one of the rooms at the club. She seemed happy, like the club was her home. It wasn't like her not to answer the phone, or let us know that her plans had changed. "Has anyone been able to reach her?"

"Not that I know of. You mind talking to this chick and see if you can get her to chill the fuck out?"

"Yeah. I'll see what I can do," I told him as I stood up and followed him back to the bar. When I picked up the phone and put it up to my ear, the line was dead. "She hung up."

"Guess it wasn't that important after all."

"Did she say who she was?"

"Nope. Just that she was looking for Tristen."

"Yeah. I guess I better see if I can figure out what's going on with her."

"Bet she found her some guy down there in Mexico. Liable to just move down there or something. Not like there's anything holding her here."

"She's got us."

"But not in the way she wants. Girls like her will always want more… and honestly, she deserves it. She's a good kid. Maybe she finally found what she's been looking for."

"Stranger things have happened, but I'll do some checking just to be sure."

"Let me know what you find out."

I went back to my room, and as soon as I logged into my computer, there was a glitch in the screen. To anyone else, it would look like nothing – just a flicker – but I knew all too well what it meant. Someone had synced a rat to one of our servers using a remote access tool. They were slick, but not slick enough to get past me. I picked up my burner and made a call to Cotton.

When he answered, I said, "We've got trouble. You better come check this out."

"I'm on my way."

As soon as I hung up, I started a counter attack. They'd only managed to crack the outer layer of my security system, so I still had time to stop them before they got into our main database. I started with an intrusion inspection, so I could find exactly where they were located. To do that, I would need their IP address. They were using an encrypted network, so all the traffic was routed through relays, making it difficult to locate them.

I was still working to find the exact address when Cotton came charging through the door. "What's wrong?"

Without looking away from my computer, I answered, "We got ourselves a hacker."

"Damn it."

Cotton leaned over me, watching as I typed away on my keyboard. Even with him breathing down the back of my neck, I managed to get the IP address. I was surprised to see it was coming from an apartment building only a few miles away. "Got him." I wrote down the address and handed it to Cotton. "We need to get someone over there, now."

"I'll send Stitch and Maverick."

"Make sure they get *everything*. Computers. Phones. Anything this guy might be using. We need to know what the hell he's after."

Cotton made the call, and once he had everything sorted, he turned back to me. "Got any idea who this guy might be?"

"No idea. I'm going to do what I can to slow him down, but I gotta tell you... whoever this is, he knows what he's doing. In a matter of minutes, he breeched my firewall."

"You gonna be able to hold him off?"

"I've got this covered. Just let me know when they get back to the club with this guy."

"You got it."

Once he was gone, I considered launching a virus, but decided to hold off. I wanted to have access to everything they had on their computer, knowing I may need it later. I bombarded their server with garbage files, making it impossible for them to get any further into our system. Going up against another hacker is like trying to solve a Rubik's Cube that keeps changing just as you get the first pattern in place. I was making headway when it became apparent that my assailant was no longer there. It wasn't long before I got word from Stitch that they'd gotten our guy and were heading back to the clubhouse. I knew where they'd be taking him. When there were questions to be answered, questions that some guys weren't so willing to answer, Stitch brought them to his playroom. It was a place where he didn't have any problems getting answers.

Knowing they'd be back any minute, I grabbed my laptop and started towards the back of the clubhouse. When I walked into the room, Maverick gave me a strange look—a look I might expect if I was about to be the brunt of some joke, not the kind I'd expect after they'd just apprehended the guy who'd just tried to hack into our database. I stopped dead in my tracks and asked, "What?"

He smirked as he motioned to a chair centered in the back of the room. "We got the big, badass hacker for ya."

His sarcasm didn't go unnoticed as I looked over to see who they'd bound to the chair. I'll admit I had my own thoughts about who our hacker could've been – maybe an old enemy that resurfaced to take his revenge, or a member of an MC that was set on taking down our club. There'd been a hundred different ideas that crossed my mind over the past hour, but never once did I ever imagine that it could've been the person sitting in that chair. I glanced back over at Maverick and growled, "You've got to be fucking kidding me."

"Nope."

I looked back over at the beautiful blonde with emerald green eyes as I ran my hand through my hair. "Well, I'll be damned."

Did you enjoy this excerpt?
Look for "Big" available on Amazon.com!

Printed in Great Britain
by Amazon